FROM GEEK TO GREEK BILLIONAIRE

DID HE DESERVE A SECOND CHANCE? COULD HE LOVE A WOMAN WITH SECRETS?

GLORIA SILK

Cover Vision by Tanya Freedman

Cover Designed by Tara Green, Fantasia Frog Designs

From Geek to Greek Billionaire/Gloria Silk—1st Edition

Published by Creative Hummingbird Results

GET HOT RELEASE NEWS AND FREE EBOOKS

I'd love to send you exclusive, exciting book news, free books and special offers. **Please subscribe on Gloria Silk's Newsletter page now: www.GloriaSilk.com**

I also love to hear from my readers, just email me: Email Gloria Silk now or after you've read this book. Your feedback is always appreciated as it helps me to constantly improve my craft and your entertainment.

~

Do you review books because you love reading good quality fiction?

Then you're someone after my own heart!

As the best way of sharing great books with others is by far word of mouth and reviews, after you've read this book, please consider reviewing it.

I love receiving your emails telling me how much you enjoyed a certain book of mine, please keep them coming, and also it would help so much if you share your thoughts on any platform where you buy books, even if it's a quick one liner that shows you've read the book you're reviewing.

Remember, good books deserve to be shared with your friends and loved ones.

~

NOBODY'S BABY BUT MINE - Available April 28, 2018

"Gripping, sensuous and astute."

Can Rachel and James find their way back into each other's hearts after tasting temptation and facing devastating news? How strong is love in the face of reality and deep desire?

Summer, 2018: Healing Love - A young artist's craving for love endangers her restaurant as well as her life. How can she turn her life around and find everlasting love?

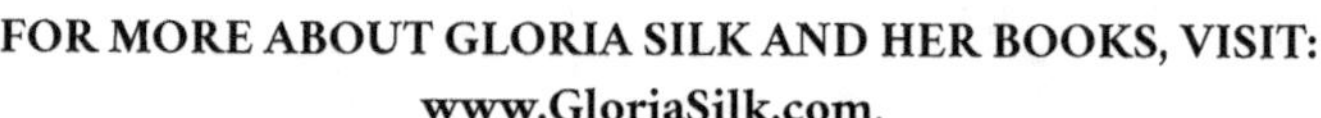

FOR MORE ABOUT GLORIA SILK AND HER BOOKS, VISIT:
www.GloriaSilk.com.

surpassed my expectations! It's wonderfully written to tell a lovely story filled with lots of emotions and authentic characters. The author did a fantastic job! I felt so close to Lia and Devraj while reading about their forbidden, but blossoming love. I found myself cheering for them! I couldn't wait to find out if their love would pull through. As a true fan of this genre, I highly recommend this book. It's one of those must-have books that you've got to get in your collection!!! *Must-Have Romance Books Reviewer*

~

5 stars - **First and Only Destiny** was amazing. This is the debut novel by Gloria Silk and I hope she writes many more, as I thoroughly enjoyed this fast paced story of first love with all the sweetness and angst that drives this coming of age experience.

What makes **First and Only Destiny** even more unique is the added complications of those two very divisive elements: culture and religion. The young lovers, Lia, is a Jewish budding beauty and art student who is instantly drawn to the divinely handsome, exotic and dashing Devraj, an Indian prince and captain of industry in the making. Lia knows that the relationship is doomed because her family will never accept anyone but a Jewish husband for her. She has seen how unrelentingly immoveable they are by how difficult they have made her favourite aunt's life because the man she is planning to marry is non-Jewish.

Devraj's family is equally inflexible, planning for him to take an Indian wife. But although they are less direct with him, his father approaches Lia directly to reject her and the notion of Devraj marrying outside his culture.

First and Only Destiny is painfully and passionately sweet as only a first love that is destined to be denied can be. It is an old story, yet new and different because of its timeliness and the skill and creativity with which Gloria Silk tells it.

Put this book on your list and get to it as soon as you can! *Yvonne Finn, Author, YourRelationshipWhisperer.com*

⁓

From the minute I started reading this book to the end I was captivated by the story line. Laughing and crying together with the characters as a story was unveiling shows how carefully and masterly each word was used in the book to affect those emotions. Hot and sexy scenes just added a nice and elegant flavour to this book. The story will keep you on your toes till you finish reading it.

Great book. Hope to see more of Gloria Silk talent. **S Yosefi**

⁓

5 stars - Oct. 14, 2016 - Wonderful romance book! I found that there was an incredible chemistry between characters. The author really brought the best of their races and cultures to light. This book reminded me of a modern-day Romeo and Juliet. Star-crossed lovers who were determined to be together forever. I would definitely recommend this book to anyone who likes a good romantic story, especially about family dynamics.

⁓

Very good read. You don't want to put it down. Really enjoyed the cultural conflicts that many families can relate to. I bought this book and **Second Destiny** from the author at a local book signing. Gloria is such a lovely, upbeat person and I love her British accent! I felt so sorry for the tough choice that Lia Abraham and Devraj Shah had to face make when they were young university students; to say goodbye and please their families, or to defy their families for love of each other. One family is Jewish, the other is Hindu.

In **Second Destiny**, an unsettling replay in the younger generation haunts Lia and Devraj, and they face another life-altering decision.

I'm so glad I bought both books at the same time to enjoy these emotionally-charged page turners. Get your hankies ready. *Joan Leacott, Author*

~

I am a huge fan of reading romance books. This book was amazing because it is an interracial romance novel. I'm in an interracial relationship myself, so this book hit home for me. Gloria Silk is an amazing author that has provided a well-written and beautiful romance. Lia is a shy art major who doesn't want anyone to come between her and her dreams. She meets Devraj and is shy around him. Lia is planning on going full force into her art career, but after one kiss from Devraj, she has been hooked. Lia is Jewish and Devraj is Hindu. It was really interesting to see them both come together and fall in love. Both of them are feeling pressure from their families, but they are truly falling in love. This book was so amazing, I read it in one sitting. I'm truly a fan of interracial romance books and this one a great find. I would highly recommend it! *Annelei C*

~

First and Only Destiny is a tale of unrequited love that begins in college and spans a short time where hearts are torn apart by family obligations. Hindu Devraj and Jewish Lia compare with Romeo and Juliet, with their families opposed to the love-match. Lia's parents want her to marry Howard. But she only loves Devraj. The college romance fills our hearts with joy and pain.

Ella and Jim are excellent friends, who back up the love of Dev and Lia. I loved the multi-cultural theme, sharing different cultures in this rich tale. Gloria Silk is an author you want to read. She tells a wonderful tale that proves that love conquers all. I highly recommend this up-and-coming author. *Franny Armstrong, Author*

~

5 stars - I could not wait to read Gloria Silk's story **First and Only Destiny** to see who's second destiny we would be talking about? Getting in to the book I was so happy the main characters came together and just as all books should engage the emotions of the reader I really got frustrated every time they would break up. As a matter of fact I put it down. Even peeked at the end. I would love to see the movie, great story! *Ellen Cohen*

~

ACKNOWLEDGMENTS

Thank you to my content and copy editors, and cover designer. You help me improve my work, and you make it shine.

This is an expanded novel which was originally published as a novella, as part of the bestselling anthology, Billionaires on the Beach, the Anderson Brothers. Many thanks to Elizabeth Lennox who invited me to be part of this incredible and uplifting—not to mention romantic—project; I was honoured to have my story *From Geek to Greek Billionaire* included as the last in the series.

I'm proud to announce that 100% of the proceeds from all five authors (Elizabeth Lennox, Noelle Adams, Leslie North and Lizabeth Scott and me) went to charity in aid of breast cancer research.

Not only was this collaboration so much fun and we helped a charity cause close to our hearts (raising over $10000), I've now got even more likeminded author friends. They don't think I'm crazy or obsessed when I talk about my created heroes as if they're real and they'll be coming over for dinner. It's no secret that I fall madly in love with all my various heroes because who doesn't fantasize about a gorgeous, smart, quick-witted and romantic man of our dreams?

That segues perfectly to my very own real-life hero; my husband of 27 years. Austin still surprises me and makes me laugh every day, and thankfully has no problem with my virtual romances with my imaginary romantic heroes. So, as always, my love and appreciation goes to my personal hero and patron of my arts, without whose unfailing support my dreams would not come true.

Thanks also go to Kate Freiman, an amazing author, mentor and friend who has always inspired and helped me stay on track and constantly strive to improve my craft. Thanks, Kate for also finding my first opening sentence for this story, which I had buried later in the page. You're truly gracious on so many levels.

Finally, my deep gratitude to all of you, my lovely readers who tell me in your most welcome emails etc., about how much you enjoy the stories, and how so many of you fall as madly in love with my heroes as I do, and wish you could meet great guys like them!

Enjoy and keep those emails and reviews coming. They're so appreciated.

*N*ine and a half years earlier

*O*livia hadn't imagined that her first time would be in a large walk-in linen closet, even if it was in a five star hotel. One tentative kiss from the shy, sweet Alexander had changed everything.

Both of them were shaking in each other's arms, the napkins they had come for lay strewn beside them by their feet.

Alexander's touch stole Olivia's breath. Everything seemed to move in slow motion. The inevitability was mesmerizing.

This shouldn't be happening...*We've only known each other a few weeks.* Six whole wonderful, romantic weeks.

But no words would come out.

Was that romantic music playing only inside *her* head?

Within minutes their world turned into a grown up paradise where only love and pleasure existed.

Enveloped within those large muscular arms, Olivia

welcomed the heat in her pulsating body as she tried to control her erratic breathing.

She smiled under Alexander's stare, grateful that he also looked as shaken up as she was.

"Olivia, wow." His low voice surrounded her in their cocoon. She loved the delicious scent of his understated cologne mingled with the smell of lemony fresh laundry.

"I...I'm sorry, Olivia. Are you OK? Did I hurt you?"

When she shook her head he sighed and added, "Good. I couldn't help myself, I love you...so much." He kissed her again and she wanted to cry from his sweetness. Her heart thrummed even faster as she looked up into his frank, green eyes. They were filled with awe as if he hadn't realized the intensity of what he felt until the words had come out.

Their incredible bond of having given each other the gift of their virginities could never be broken. She felt it in her bones and saw it clearly in his face that Alexander was in the same exact nirvana.

As if psychic, he whispered into her temple, his warmth breath sending shivers of delight through her body, "You know I love you very much, right, Olivia? So much...it hurts. This isn't just..."

She nodded and smiled, blinking tears away to enjoy the vision of the adoration in his eyes. In his arms she felt absolutely beautiful, not overweight or clumsy, or geeky.

Everything felt so perfect, so right.

She could imagine meeting his large family, those Anderson boys and the parents. She visualized how much her parents and her younger sister, Lisa would love this humble, shy yet amazing guy.

But there was no rush for any of that. At eighteen she was still in college to pursue interior design, and he was considering his options right here in Wrightsville Beach or in his birth country, Greece.

"I can't wait to show you off at the gala tomorrow." Alexander's deep slow laugh reverberated within his chest straight into her heart.

"You make me so happy, Olivia. I could never imagine feeling like this about anyone in the world." His lips trailed her temple to her ear, then from her cheek to her mouth.

Another kiss to seal their love. It was magical.

She was about to admit her love for him when the loud knock on the door jarred her.

"Hey, Alexander, are you there? Where'd you disappear to?" Brittany's nasal voice broke through their haven.

Cool air met Olivia's exposed upper body, making her shiver.

Alexander sighed and with a regretful expression let her go. "Be there shortly." He called out. Then he helped her with her with her blouse before adjusting his own clothing.

"This summer, today, they've been the most important times of my life. You're unforgettable. My Olivia."

She felt her lower lip tremble again as she kept her happy tears at bay and smiled. They would see each other later and she would tell him that she loved him too.

It would all work out, she just knew it.

~

*W*hat *a difference a few moments make.* Alex tried to calm himself and not grin like a romantic oaf. Making love with the luscious, beautiful, red-haired Olivia had been even more incredible than he had dreamed or imagined.

He strode towards the brightly lit banquet hall, his hands laden with the large mountain of white napkins from the linen closet. He knew his life would never be the same again and through her expressive eyes he felt confident that Olivia shared his feelings in precisely the same way. She hadn't said much because it had all happened so fast. She was probably speechless.

It had felt so damn good. And next time when they were together it would be in a real bed....

He bit his inner lip to stop grinning. He could never have enough of Olivia.

"So." He jumped as Brittany materialized from behind him. Trying to control his equilibrium he shed the heavy pile of linens on the table beside him and turned to face her.

"I see she got what she'd wanted." Brittany said, her overly-made-up cat-like brown eyes boring into his.

"What are you talking about?" He looked away for a moment but she entered his personal space.

"I'm talking about you and Olivia in the closet. She must have played the virgin act so well."

"Stop, Brittany. I don't want to hear anything—"

"Okay, have it your way." Brittany flicked her blonde hair and started turning away, then added, "As your friend I thought you should know that I heard Brad saying to someone that he was going to the gala with Olivia."

Alexander stood very still. Showing no emotion he forced himself to breathe normally. "You've got your facts wrong. But thanks for your concern." He swiveled away from her, but she clutched his arm.

"Why don't you ask her?"

Although he wouldn't look at her he stayed immobile.

She added, "You see? You know it in your gut. Maybe she'll deny it, or maybe she'll tell you the truth. That she was using you to make Brad jealous."

It didn't make sense to him, because he'd never seen Olivia or Brad speak or even acknowledge each other.

Or maybe he'd just been a fool all along.

CHAPTER 1

The present

Olivia loved dogs, but that huge monstrosity galloping towards her was definitely not a mere dog. Before she could take action, she was whisked out of its way and unceremoniously dumped onto the hot sand centimeters out of the barking black beast's path. Her breath caught as a big weight held her in place.

Olivia tasted grit in her dry mouth as something wet and rough sniffed at her cheek. "Off Spartacus," someone called above her. Within seconds strong hands drew her to her feet as she saw the large dog and his owner continue on their way down the shore.

"Are you okay?" The deep voice held a certain urgency.

Her pride and ego were the only things that were hurt. Straightening, she flicked her hair out of her burning face and stared up at her tall, bearded savior. He was regarding her through the lenses of black-framed glasses, with a combination of concern and curiosity.

She nodded but no words came out.

The expression in the man's striking green eyes suddenly changed. He let her go and his eyes widened. "I—I'm glad." And added, "Olivia? Olivia Moore?"

Frowning, she nodded again and then recognition snatched her breath for the second time, the emotional impact even more powerful than her encounter with the hot sand.

"I'm Alexander, Alex Anderson." His black beard and thick curly hair had changed his appearance, but as soon as she looked into those eyes again she knew him. Her best friend's brother-in-law, who now lived in Greece. And worse, her secret, unrequited teenage crush. Well, not so secret….

This couldn't be happening.

His earnest gaze boring into her, he said, "We knew each other when we worked on the gala—"

"I remember," she said hastily. "Well, thanks for . . . you know." She swept a trembling hand at nothing in particular.

Olivia stepped back, intent on getting away from him as quickly as possible without humiliating herself by breaking into a dead run.

Without warning, he grabbed her shoulders and pulled her hard against him again just as a bike whooshed inches away, its bell tinkling belatedly.

She felt the broad muscles hidden by Alexander's baggy navy-blue sweatshirt. He smelled as fresh and welcoming as he had on that night when they had kissed and . . .

The night that had changed her life and he had disappeared without a word.

"Okay, I'm definitely not this unlucky, or this clumsy!"

As soon as she started to back away from him, desperate to be free of his touch, he released her. She would not think about how red her face and neck were right now against her darned red hair. Why was she born to love the sun and the beach when they made her appear like a cooked lobster no matter how much sun protection she used?

She picked up her large brimmed sun hat, dusted it off, and pulled her white muslin over-shirt closer around her body.

"Thanks again. Bye."

"You're welcome, but wait up. How have you been?"

"I don't want to be rude, but I'd rather not chit-chat with the guy who stood me up on one of the most important nights in my life, especially after we…"

After they had made love and Alexander had told her he loved her.

What else had he said a lifetime ago in that huge hotel linen closet?

You make me so happy, Olivia. I could never imagine feeling like this about anyone in the world.

"What do you mean?" Alexander frowned, his dark brows like crows' wings above his bright green eyes. "You're the one who—"

"It doesn't matter, honestly. Have a good life." She turned, checked that nothing else was bearing down on her, and escaped towards the beach house, affectionately named the Ellis cottage. Renovating the quaint beach house was the reason she was back here in Wrightsville Beach. And she was on a deadline.

As he strode beside her, Alexander's hand touched her forearm. She halted and glared at it until he released her. She turned to face him and found him studying her, his expression solemn.

"Olivia, I did *not* stand you up, and if you just stop a moment we can sort it out."

Olivia stood still, worried her lower lip and was glad her hair covered most of her face and her curiosity.

He was probably in Wrightsville Beach visiting his family, which meant she would either have this conversation now or avoid him all over town.

Oh, did her best friend, Maria know that he was here? "Okay,

I'm listening. But..." She glanced towards the nearby café, "I need some water."

Weaving their way around the locals and jovial, tan tourists worshipping the sun they reached the popular Wilmington café. Olivia recoiled at the scent of hot dogs and deli sandwiches. Why had she delayed her daily jog to the middle of the morning? She liked the quiet of the early mornings with no temptation or distraction.

"May I get you something else?" When she shook her head Alexander nodded, handed her one bottle and paid for their waters before she got her change ready.

"Thanks."

As they sat in the welcome shade under the sun-umbrella in the early May heat, Alexander studied her with those deep green eyes behind his glasses until she forgot what they had been talking about. His level gaze took her right back to that night. The tingles all over her body made her feel strangely lethargic and warm inside. She forced herself to focus on his words.

"Brittany told me that you were going to the gala with Brad," he said quietly. "That you'd been trying to make him jealous."

Stunned, she barely managed an indignant protest. "Me? With *Brad*? And Brittany and I were not the best of friends." Understatement of the century. The blonde had disliked her on sight no matter how Olivia tried to win her over during their weeks working on the charity event together.

He nodded and glanced away for a moment, then shrugged. "I should have realized that, but..."

"How could you believe that Brad would even know I existed? He'd never be seen with a pudgy girl like me. And there *was* such a thing as the phone even in those days, you know." Oh, God, she sounded like she still cared. She shrugged and drank some more of her ice cold water.

Studying his face she became certain they both knew that Brittany had been her nemesis and that it had been his excuse, his way out. Perhaps when the sexual haze had lifted he had thought it through and realized they shouldn't have done anything in the first place.

"I'd hoped, I thought we'd go together, but…" Even as his voice trailed into silence, he scanned her face. She couldn't tear her gaze away from that deep curiosity she remembered within those eyes…. that pulled her into his orbit.

"You left without saying a word, just disappearing to Greece."

"I'm sorry." He glanced away for a moment.

Despite her memories of his leaving and her disappointment and heartbreak, her thoughts took her back to their time together, and Olivia suddenly felt hungry, not for food but for his sweet, hesitant kisses that she still remembered so well. Even after nearly ten years.

She forced her attention away, focusing on a laughing toddler riding his tricycle up the path, his mother scurrying behind.

Aware of Alexander's gaze still on her, she relented and offered him an olive branch.

"It was such a success, I wish you'd seen all our hard work come to fruition," she admitted.

They had met when Aunt Jenny, her best friend's grand-mother, had organized the big event for the "Deaf and Blind Children" charity. When the tall, lanky and unassuming guy with slouching shoulders came to volunteer, Olivia immediately felt their shared kinship for helping others. And for not being eligible for the in-crowd.

"I'm so sorry I missed it. When I thought back I realized that you never told me that you loved me—" Did he actually blush? Olivia couldn't tell through the beard, but just the tops of his cheeks seemed flushed as he continued, "And neither did you confirm that we would go together. But I should have—"

She shook her head. "It's okay." What else could she say?

You broke my naive little heart. I felt like an idiot for believing every word you said. I vowed never to trust any guy from then on...

"At least now I know why you didn't attend. It was better that way in the long run. We were too young and we come from different worlds." She stood up, tried to smile and failed.

"I don't understand what you mean—"

"None of that matters. It was…good bumping into you, but I've got to go. I'm helping Maria redesign and update her grandmother's beach house."

The hint of amusement in his eyes and the slight curve of those sensuous lips—which had been the first to kiss hers—made her suddenly uneasy yet curious.

"Still helping others before helping yourself?"

Pushing away memories of the insistent dreams of their delicious kisses and union she concentrated on his words. "I'm an interior designer. It's what I do for a living. And despite Maria being my best friend, I'm getting well paid." So why did she feel like a defensive teenager, flushing and feeling the heat that had nothing to do with the North Carolina weather?

Remember you're here to do a job and then move on, with no distractions. No meandering down any memory lane!

Even if he had meant his words of love at the time in that linen closet, he had still run. Had she thought he was different from any twenty-year-old with raging hormones? Maybe that was all it had been for them both.

"Great. I should have known you'd be the designer of Maria's project. I hope we'll bump—ah—see more of each other."

Not if I can help it, she nearly said, but shut her mouth before the words came out.

"I thought you live in Greece now." She felt her cheeks burn again, "Not that I'd asked or anything, it just came up in conversation." She would rather eat scorpions than admit that Maria had updated her on all of her youngest brother-in-law's work and romantic adventures until two years ago. When Sofia DeLongi had come into Alexander's life, something had changed within Olivia.

Hope and naivety had fled.

Tall, stick-thin with glossy black hair that touched that pert derrière, Sofia, Olivia admitted to herself, was the perfect mate for Alexander. Clamping down, Olivia had finally stopped her best friend from elaborating on anything to do with him.

If not for her unavoidable surgery three and a half years ago, Olivia was certain she would have witnessed him with one of his earlier gorgeous girlfriends at Maria's and Sloan's wedding. Only Maria knew the true reason Olivia was absent on her best friend's special day. And it had nothing to do with Alexander, or any other man. It was about survival.

"So I suppose you're visiting family?" Olivia focused on the present.

"Yes." He broke their eye contact, like he used to when they had first met. He had always been quiet but now seemed even more so. Inexplicably enigmatic and now even more sexy!

He had grown into a handsome man.

No matter how attractive he was in his understated and geeky way, she would not care why Alexander was here. He would probably return to his life in Greek paradise within a few days. They were no longer stupid, romantic youths who had shared a first kiss and lost their virginities to each other.

Alexander may have been her first love, but he certainly would not be her only love, she was sure. Now as a twenty-seven-year-old she had long discarded her rose-tinted glasses and saw the world clearly.

Her burgeoning career took up every waking moment and that was the way she liked her life.

She was determined to continue growing her brand and regain the industry's trust after those few years of lost opportunities.

Alexander was part of her past, and that was where he would stay.

~

*A*lex could not believe how strangely he felt just by looking into Olivia's large blue eyes. They seemed even more knowing yet reserved, and understandably so.

Olivia Moore was here now, when he needed peace and quiet and to think clearly. He felt like his twenty-year-old self; gawky, unsure of himself and unworthy of someone as lovely and generous as Olivia.

She appeared to be as gregariously colorful and full of life, with her burning red wavy hair and those huggable, sinfully delicious curves covered sensuously in a tight sports top, pants and over shirt.

Well, he was going to regroup and see how he could make this gift work to his advantage. He *had* been a coward all those years ago; he should have sought her out before or even during the gala and demanded answers from his first love.

But like his brothers had always teased him, he had turned chicken and run.

Unable to take his eyes off her, he heard her repeat how busy her life was, but all he could think about was the night before the gala, when their kisses had turned from explorative to explosive passion.

How alive he felt just remembering that time.

Ah, that large, warm hotel linen closet. Ever since that day, the lemony, lavender scents of fresh linens transported him back to their first time.

From the first moment he saw her, he had been attracted to her generous spirit. Then he could not resist that voluptuous body and those delicious breasts, which had driven him crazy.

But she had been adamant that she was an overweight geek.

Even when he had tried to tell her how beautiful she was, she hadn't heard him. She never noticed how the other boys had stared at her, but *he* certainly had. Instead of confessing and repeating what he really felt about her mind and her delectable body, he had determined to prove to her how desirable she was.

Finally, as a naïve and shy twenty-year-old he had gotten carried away....And had ruined it all afterwards.

Now he was at the right place at the right time, here at the beach, where the fun-loving Aunt Jenny had first befriended him. Who would have guessed that Aunt Jenny's granddaughter, Maria, would become his first sister-in-law?

Seeing Olivia here, he was glad to be back. His gut, which had helped and saved him many times in business over the past decade, told him that Maria—and somehow Aunt Jenny—were the reasons why he was here.

If his romantic sister-in-law had engineered his return to Wrightsville Beach to rekindle his romance with her best friend, he hoped it meant that Olivia was unattached.

Propelled by a force he could not resist he was determined to utilize all his business acumen and win her trust back. Perhaps he could ask some of his happily married brothers and their wives for some overdue advice about how he could get to know Olivia once more without screwing it up again.

CHAPTER 2

"Why didn't you tell me that Alexander was in town?" Olivia asked Maria as she entered the Ellis cottage she was in charge of redesigning and renovating. The cool, white, two-bedroom beach house was now extended to have three-bedrooms and two bathrooms.

"I thought you didn't care to hear anything about him ever again." Maria's smirk and sparkling eyes were too perceptive for Olivia.

"I still don't care, I'd have just liked a bit of notice. I bumped into him—literally—on the beach. Like in those cliché movies. I must look such a sight." Cringing, she shared what happened earlier.

"I'm sure it wasn't all that bad. And anyway, you've always loved J-Lo in 'The Wedding Planner,'" Maria was almost laughing now. "So how did you feel seeing your first love after…how long?"

"Nine and half years. And he was nothing more than a silly crush."

Glancing behind her at the various workers around them Maria almost whispered, "You did lose your virginity to him, and they say the first one is always special."

"Not true." Olivia turned away in the large, open-plan living area to study the workmanship and progress of one of the men painstakingly priming the original ship lap on the ceilings and the wainscoting. "Any way, what do you think about my suggested fabrics for Aunt Jenny's armchair and ottoman? And you have to decide on the wallpaper today, please, Maria."

"Yes, let's change the subject and jump straight into work, like always." Maria's amusement was getting too much for her now.

With her fists on her hips Olivia said slowly, "Maria, you know so much more than anyone has a right to know about me and my past, but I'd really appreciate you helping me stay on track with this house. *You* gave me the July 31 deadline, remember? And please help me find a way to stop thinking about— being distracted by anything other than my work." At Maria's arched look she added in a defensive tone, "Alexander and I don't belong in each other's worlds, and he may well be married or with another Sofia DeLongi, for all I know."

Maria burst out laughing, "Kid yourself, everyone, but not me. You know he's single since Sofia left him for his third cousin last year."

Olivia had known that but perhaps some new models had sprouted on to the scene since then, and from what she'd seen at the beach, he was way hotter than he had been at nearly twenty-one. He had broadened and become a real man's man, even in unflattering baggy clothes. Her imagination caused her to wonder what they were hiding. She felt that warmth all over her body and gripped the sample books tighter within her hands.

"Maybe this is a good opportunity to revisit what you had together. I want you to be as happy as I am with Sloan, and the rest of the Anderson—"

"I don't have the time or inclination for any of that, Maria." Olivia blinked and forced her imagination to stop running away with itself. She felt ashamed at how easily she was already distracted and how tempting her friend's suggestion sounded.

She shook her head. "As I say, let's get this project done. Let's stage the beach house, add the fantabulous photos and videos of it to my portfolio and my website, and let me move on to my next adventure."

"Don't worry, Liv." Maria neared her and put her arms around her. Her eyes weren't sparkling like they had a moment ago. "I promise you that you'll be even more successful than you were before. It wasn't your fault you had to fight and conquer…all the stuff you went through. But you can still have some fun. You deserve happiness and I know you'll get it, including your business success. You're one strong girl and you're the most talented designer in the whole world."

Trying to push the sudden tears away, Olivia dropped the sample books on the nearby table and hugged Maria hard, saying, "Not that you're biased or trying to get the best discount you can out of me."

Staring at each other, Olivia gave Maria a tremulous smile.

"Yep, that's what I'm all about," said the friend who was married to one of the sexiest and most successful billionaires in the country. "You'll be absolutely fine, Liv, I promise you'll never feel alone. I love you."

"I love you, too." At this, Olivia didn't stop her tears. She knew she was still reeling from seeing the damned geek. She was so attracted to his enigmatic air and inner strength, and how he had transformed into a broad-chested god from the shy young man she remembered.

She would have to forget all about her silly schoolgirl crush, that was all, and concentrate on her work at hand.

"I'm so lucky to have you, Maria, so now earn your friendship and help me. I cannot be distracted." Then once again picking up the fabric and wallpaper samples for the final rooms, she entered into her favorite world of design. "And this time, *please* make your choice. The extension is almost done and we have to make timely decisions to stay on track. You can't keep telling me, 'what would *you* like to see here if you lived here?' Because it's your home—no, don't remind me that you're selling it." Olivia warned her friend.

"I have a good idea. Let's choose them together, Liv."

Olivia smiled as she shook her head as they started going through the samples.

~

*A*lex discovered from Sloan, through Maria, that Olivia usually took her morning run in the early, quieter hours along the beach path hugging the long shore.

He zigzagged his way to jog beside Olivia who nearly tripped at his sudden appearance.

"Hope you don't mind the company," he said, even though her body language and the frown over her huge sunglasses confirmed that she disliked the idea immensely. He kept his eyes focused on the sandy path ahead of them, but was only too aware of how Olivia's perfect breasts danced within their constrained, sky blue sports-top. And how her glorious, thick red ponytail bobbed from side to side across her shoulder blades. Although her flushed cheeks told him she may have been running for a while, she didn't seem out of breath.

"Actually, this is my morning time when I like to think and brainstorm. I don't mean to be rude." Olivia said staring ahead, her chin rising slightly.

He didn't like her sunglasses covering her expressive eyes. "No offence taken. But I need your help. Perhaps we can set up a short meeting as soon as possible. It's a personal, sensitive subject."

"Why me?" Flashing him a sideways glance she immediately

focused on the path ahead. Had her cheeks grown even more rosy?

Her soft rhythmical breathing made him wonder what she would sound like when making love. He couldn't remember that part from their first time, damn it. *Stop being so crass, you're no animal.*

Oh, yes, his mission. "I can explain it in private, when you have a few minutes."

Was that curiosity or her searching for a way to get rid of him?

"Okay, I'll bite, let's take a few minutes now. Shoot." She stopped at a bench by some big pink flowering bushes.

He stood next to her as she stretched, admiring her curves and suppleness. When she faced him, he was about to reach for her sunglasses when she took them off.

"I'm listening." She arched a light eyebrow. Staring into her blue eyes, he nearly forgot his plan. Would she see through him?

Even though he was not biologically related to his four brothers, their bond was indestructible. It still amazed him how Grey, his playboy brother, who was ten months older than him, had fallen so completely and deeply for Gemma over two years ago. Not only did Alex trust Grey's business skills, he could divulge anything to him and Grey would keep their secret and help whichever way he could.

But talking with him last night had not helped.

Sure, Grey had refrained from laughing at Alex's clumsiness in the romance department, but he realized that he had to find his own way forward. Both Grey and the ever-protective Sloan challenged him to get a grip and grow up, and go for it.

He loved his brothers to death, but a fat lot of good they were telling him what he already knew! And no doubt his mother would flat out tell him to stop hiding behind his work and settle with the right girl just like the rest of his siblings had.

While here he was stumbling like a teenager over his words, unable to openly ask Olivia out for coffee, never mind a date.

Shaking himself inwardly, he knew he couldn't do it.

Coward.

He said, "I'd like your help. I really like this woman, but I've not had the guts to approach her. Before you ask, my brothers and their well-meaning spouses would not get what my issue really is. You knew me back when and know what I was like. You're the only person I trust to understand who I am inside."

She shook her head, "But your ex-girl-friend—" He couldn't help interrupting her, not wanting to hear anything about Sofia or any other girls.

"Please hear me out, Olivia. I'm not talking about giving me a makeover like a suit, or contact lenses—I don't ever want to try those again—but the whole package, starting on the inside."

Olivia's eyes darkened, she stiffened and then the flush on her cheeks grew to her whole face and seeped towards her cleavage.

Oh no! What had he said?

"You believe that I'm the only other . . . geek, an overweight one at that, who'll be a good pal and show you how to win over another one of those . . . ." With fists by her thighs she seemed like she was about to be launched out of a cannon.

"You're not overweight, you're beau—"

"Not anymore, but you probably still see me the same way."

Was that pain he saw through the anger sparkling in her eyes? She started to turn away from him.

"No, not at all. I never saw you that way.... Let me explain properly. Please." He waited while his heart beat like he was the idiot who was about to lose Olivia again.

Although she did not sit, at least she was still listening, biting her lower lip like she used to when under pressure.

"I know that you think I've had all sorts of girlfriends, but they had either been casual dates for special occasions. . . . And Sofia actually approached me and it went on from there. I no longer want to be reactive, but proactive. I want to choose and get to know the woman *I'm* interested in." He pointed to himself and added, "I believe, in those couple of months nearly ten years ago, you really got to know the real me, that we had something that some friends and lovers don't ever get."

"I've grown up. How do you know that I haven't changed and become untrustworthy?" Her blush now seemed to hold a tinge of warmth without the anger of moments ago.

"Have you?"

She didn't reply but looked away from him. "Sorry. I'd help if I thought I was capable, but I don't have the time or...the inclination."

"Olivia, I just want to have a trusted friend who can show me what a woman really wants and not what my family thinks I should or shouldn't say or do. I have every faith that you *can* help me. Please consider it, it would mean a lot to me. Here's my offer; I'll pay you and you can do with the money what you want, put it towards your business, or towards charity like you always like to do." At this Olivia's widened eyes focused on his face.

"But," he continued, "you must promise that you'll be honest with me on all counts and that this arrangement will stay solely between us."

He handed her his business card with his private cell number handwritten on it, and left her before she could refuse again. He started a slow jog in the opposite direction from her, saying over his shoulder, "I'll be in touch tomorrow, Olivia."

CHAPTER 3

"Thanks for sharing all sorts of things about me with Alexander." Olivia couldn't help sounding hurt. She absently rubbed the adorable dog's ears, as Ollie, the large mutt gave her a most friendly and welcoming greeting. The lovable dog seemed to know she needed extra reassurance and nuzzles from her namesake. Especially after the completely opposite reaction of the huge, black-curly canine that had nearly trampled Olivia yesterday on the beach.

"What kinds of things? Just because he's my brother-in-law, I'd never divulge any personal information, Liv." Maria's frown confirmed to Olivia that she had overreacted.

"Sorry. Would Sloan by any chance know about my work with charity or about my business?"

"Ah, yes, of course I've talked with Sloan about your various work. I'm proud of my BFF, but remember, you met Alexander while you were both volunteering for a charity. And I'm sure he's also looked you up online." Then the sparkle in Maria's darker blue eyes returned, "So, how's it going with him?"

"Alexander wants to hire me…for some consultation work." But before Maria could ask anything else, Olivia changed the subject. "But anyway, that doesn't matter. The electrician is due at eleven o'clock, and then the plumber will be finished with the bathroom and the new shower room. I'll keep an eye on him so he doesn't delay anymore. Otherwise…"

"Vittorio wouldn't dare let you down after you had a 'word' with him the other day. Anyway, about Alexander and you." Maria wouldn't let her interrupt, "What exactly would he like your help with?"

"It's confidential, and I'm not sure I'll be able to—"

"Don't let your pride get in the way of business. With so much talent at his disposal, if he's asking you for help, I'd consider accepting his offer. We both know the extra income will be a godsend to you right now. I know you're doing much better, but every little helps. And God knows I wouldn't dream of offering to help you financially after you nearly threatened me bodily harm at the suggestion."

"Thank you for your opinion. Now, did the electrician turn up?" Olivia asked, feeling less sure about her decision to decline his strange offer for the sake of keeping away from him. When she saw him, memories of her own 'slightly' overweight self drew out her melancholy side. Only reminding herself of her new friend, Gemma's helpful encouragement over the past couple of weeks helped her get a grip. Her best friend's latest sister-in-law was becoming her own good friend to whom she had divulged about her past health challenges. Unlike many friends and even relatives, the word cancer hadn't scared off the woman. Gemma's openness, warmth and passion for helping people had broken down many of Olivia's barriers from the moment they had met. Loving Zumba as much as Maria and Gemma did, she joined them whenever she had a chance. Gemma's thriving gym was a local hub renowned for many a-blossomed friendship and successful transformations.

While Ollie lounged in a shaded area in the back yard, over the next few hours Olivia and Maria discussed the progress of the project. Then Maria checked her cell and realized the time. "I have to go, Liv," She said with regret in her voice and her face. "Sandra's babysitting Tyler and Jordan."

Olivia smiled. Maria and Sloan's adorable two-year-old Tyler and Gemma and Grey's seven-month-old Jordan were no doubt being spoiled rotten by their doting grandmother.

"You and Gemma are so lucky to have such an incredible mother-in-law."

"Sandra always tells us that her grandkids keep her young," Maria smiled. "She insists on babysitting her grandchildren as often as possible, especially when her boys and their families visit."

Olivia knew that whenever they spent time in Wrightsville Beach, Sandra encouraged her respective sons and daughters-in-law to have frequent 'dates' to keep the love and romance flourishing.

"I don't blame her for loving and enjoying Tyler and Jordan so much. Kiss both those cherubs for me, and see you tomorrow bright and early." They hugged before Maria rushed off with the ever-obedient Ollie by her side.

Olivia was in her element here. Aunt Jenny had maintained her small early 1900s beach house and, despite the damage caused by the more recent hurricanes, she had lived the rest of her years in the cottage overlooking the sea.

Olivia missed her so much, and knew that Aunt Jenny would have been so proud of the resurrection and the extended part of the house.

The once rudimentary fireplaces were now gorgeous focal points in the living area and in two of the three bedrooms.

When Olivia had spent some time over the summers here as a teenager with Maria, warm and funny Aunt Jenny had adopted her as if she were her long lost granddaughter.

Thank goodness Maria had generously shared her grandmother's affections.

Transforming and updating Aunt Jenny's home to its former glory was more than her passion, and repaying the special woman's kindness and unconditional affection. She was honored that Maria had waited for her these couple of years so they could restore the Ellis cottage together.

Shortly after her breast cancer treatments were all behind her she lost her mother and then a few months after that her father died, too. Olivia had stayed to look after her younger sister Lisa and their small house in Arlington. They had only one distant aunt who had been there for them, and Olivia had learned first-hand what it meant to grow up fast. Suddenly all adult responsibilities for herself and her then nineteen-year-old sister rested solely on her shoulders.

Now that Lisa was settled in her second year of college and was becoming more self sufficient, Olivia had accepted Maria's invitation to come and help redesign the beach house. Her design company was growing and gaining great reviews and recommendations, but it was not quite at the stage where she had hoped it would be after two years.

This project was a bonus because it gave her more time to spend quality hours and days time Maria and now her new friend, Gemma, too.

She loved visualizing the potential of the beach house, planning the extension and renovation and then making it happen.

Olivia stared at the chaos around her and saw it all in her mind's eye, perfectly polished and ready for a family to move in and enjoy for years to come.

She wouldn't dwell on the fact that it was going up for sale. Maria didn't need it, as she and Sloan already had their own family beach house. They wanted to offer Aunt Jenny's cottage to a family who would enjoy it. Wishing she could one day have a similar home only made Olivia miss Aunt Jenny and her parents even more.

She inhaled a positive breath and sighed with a smile. *Positive thoughts only.*

Now, for the current state of affairs, *what would Aunt Jenny suggest I do about the shy Alexander's offer?*

The question followed her all day.

Picking up the blueprints and the agreed-upon fabric swatches Olivia ascended to the top floor to check on the tile setter's progress in the new master en-suite shower-room.

CHAPTER 4

"I've thought about it. And I'm considering doing it," Olivia said, and Alex forced himself not to give a triumphant fist pump. "But," Olivia added, "Let's go through your requirements and my rules to avoid any misunderstandings."

He nodded, still reeling from gratitude at Olivia's generous nature. She still seemed uneasy but appeared more open to helping him.

Watching the waves lap the quiet shore, they sipped the cold white wine he had generously brought with the two large glasses. How thoughtful the classy guy was. From the large grassy area at the back of Aunt Jenny's beach house the setting sun threw a warm glow over Olivia's gorgeous face, and her dark green wrap dress highlighted those luscious curves. He had so much to be grateful for, especially for having known Aunt Jenny all those years ago. Otherwise he would have never met Olivia and fallen in love with her.

Once again, he thanked his lucky stars for Maria's grandmother, for helping him come out of his shell over the years since he was a small boy, before he left for Greece.

Aunt Jenny had taught him how to appreciate life and not take its privileges for granted, and how to pay it forward. The eccentric woman had been such a romantic, regaling him with intriguing stories about her past and what could be if only people believed in their potential and life's possibilities.

His memories of Aunt Jenny always instilled within him a sense of calm. Thanks to her, he valued all his American and his biological Greek families. She had explained and answered his many questions about the complexities of family dynamics. He hadn't felt comfortable enough as a thirteen-year-old to ask his generous adoptive parents, Sandra and Jason the burning question about why his Greek father had not come back for him until he was almost grown.

Thanks to Aunt Jenny his resentment and confusion were short lived and he had spent all his summer months with his Greek family. Those were incredible times, living with his biological father in the large house overlooking the bay of the small fishing village in Porto Heli.

With so many cousins, aunts, uncles and his paternal grandmother, the scowling, elderly widow, Yaya Christina, Alex had added many more jigsaw pieces to the puzzle of his childhood. How Alex's father was so devastated at the loss of his beautiful wife, Costa Kyriakou that had been unable to function, never mind bring up a three-year-old son.

The time spent together with Aunt Jenny had been very special until at twenty, on the day of the gala Alex had decided to move to Greece permanently.

Okay, I hightailed it out of here.

Now, sitting here with Olivia, he knew he couldn't delve into the past, but he so wanted to share his new, adult life with her; to include her in it going forward.

Or had she moved on?

He would do whatever it took to get Olivia to spend time with him, even if it was under these pretenses. He needed to get to know her and reclaim her trust. He refused to acknowledge that she could discover his ploy and he would lose her trust irrevocably.

"So let's discuss your needs."

OK, back to business, as usual.

"I think an hour or two a day in the evenings will be good." He studied her trying not to betray his inner excitement at the prospect of spending time with her. "For the next six weeks until I leave. And I'll cover all expenses in addition to this amount." Alex offered her a piece of paper with a number on it.

She blinked and stared at his offered compensation. "Are you serious? There are too many zeros here."

"I'd like your commitment—outside of your work hours, of course—and we can discuss the number if you change your mind and if you want to charge me more along the way. After all, you haven't heard my needs yet."

Olivia put down her wine glass and stared at him.

He hoped he wasn't frightening her away. "It's simple. I know what I want, and I'll do anything you suggest which you think will get...her attention."

"I won't pretend to be your girlfriend or anything like that."

"No, no need for that." He shook his head, "But this is a very special woman who's very stubborn and I need to deal with her very carefully, as I don't want to lose her." He nearly said 'again.'

❀

*O*livia's heart thumped and she hated her mind playing tricks on her. She was actually wishing Alexander meant she was the girl he was talking about.

Keep on dreaming, romantic fool.

Seeing Maria and Gemma so blissfully happy was obviously tinting her reality.

Yes, true love was possible.

But not everyone was fated for the happy-ever-after romance.

And Alexander had made it clear that he saw *her* as his trusty pal from their younger, geeky and awkward years. He had opened up to her, taking for granted that she would help him like he obviously expected her to help anyone else.

Good old Olivia.

Suddenly she knew she couldn't do this. "Why not talk to Maria? She's very discreet and trustworthy. I can vouch for her. I'm sorry, I shouldn't have agreed. I'm—I'm not the best person for this."

"Please, Olivia, I know I can trust Maria, but I don't want anyone else to help me, just you. My gut has never been wrong." Before she said anything else, he asked, "Where would you suggest we start? Imagine it from her point of view. That's all I want," he looked almost desperate.

Olivia looked away from his face. "But we may be very different, with opposite priorities—this girl and I." Sighing, Olivia watched the last of the blood-orange sun disappear into the romantic horizon. Why had she agreed to help him in the first place?

"I don't think so."

"What's stopping you from asking her out right now? Is she here, is that why you're in town?"

"I—I haven't asked her out yet. We know each other from...afar, but I want to get a woman's perspective on what I've been doing wrong all these years."

As she studied his face, Olivia wondered if he was remembering his quick escape to Greece all those years ago. She still couldn't quite understand what had happened. But what was the difference, anyway?

"And how to get to know her and discover what I can offer her." He lowered his head with those lovely black curls and added, "This is not easy for me to admit to anyone. If you're game, I'll do anything you say, appearance wise, etc., and I'll answer any questions you have."

Instead of saying, *but I'm also a woman, and you're very eloquent with me*, she said, "But it's not solely about her, you have to find out if she can make you happy, too." As he seemed to consider this, she added, "Apart from some tweaks like shortening your beard and updating your wardrobe, the main work will be with the inner boost of your self-confidence, I suppose." She couldn't believe she was saying this out loud. But part of her couldn't wait to see what he looked like under those casual oversize sports pants and baggy sweat shirt.

Scanning his face, Olivia wondered if she was insulting him but was gratified to see his eager nod.

"Yes, that's exactly what I need. It's very astute of you. You see? A woman's—*your* perspective—is all I need. Thank you, Olivia." He put down his empty wine glass on the bistro table next to hers.

The pragmatic and practical part of her confirmed that Maria was right, and that the money would immensely help her and her sister's future. As long as she kept up Lisa's college payments and got back home to Arlington, Virginia, by end of July everything would stay under control.

What could be the harm in helping him?

~

"*A*bout my rules." She said firmly, trying to keep all this professional, even though she was undertaking such an intimate makeover. "I don't think it'll take more than a week. We don't need to see each other after you've asked her out. That's all you wanted, correct?" When he nodded, even despite his obvious disappointment, she went on, "In the meantime, you won't call me at all hours of the day or turn up here or at my hotel room at will. You won't expect me to go out with you unless it's unavoidable."

Was that a twinge of amusement in those green eyes? They

gravitated lower to her mouth and desire burned in them when he finally made eye contact again.

She felt a warmth build within her and hoped her blush was not betraying her inner emotions.

"A month."

"Sorry?" What had they been discussing?

"I believe you're here till the end of July. I'm around for another few weeks."

About to refuse, ready to stand up and run, Olivia took a slow deep breath and reminded herself that Alexander was obviously not as confident or as ready as she hoped he would be.

"Okay, if you really will need it." As the word left her lips he leaned closer to her and took her hand in both of his.

"I'll be forever grateful for your help, Olivia." As he looked into her eyes she wished for a crazy moment that he would lean closer and kiss her ravenous lips.

What the heck had she got herself into?

CHAPTER 5

Their time together over the next few days became a routine. Over the next week, Olivia began to look forward to their late afternoon or evening walks.

Her days started at 6a.m. to fit in her forty-five-minute run and plan the day's work at the beach house, and think of the questions she would ask Alexander that evening. With so much happening on site, her work hours rushed by.

Yesterday had been a very special time when Olivia's team of contractors finished installing the new roof, new windows and this coming week the hardwood and ceramic flooring would be completed throughout.

By end of next week the kitchen would be decked out with swish new appliances.

Then Maria and Olivia would have the fun of reallocating the reupholstered and new furniture in their intended places. The interior decorating and final touches would make this work in progress a finished, livable abode once more.

She appreciated how Maria kept including her in the design choices throughout the project. Maria had wonderful taste and had done a fabulous job with designing and finishing her and Sloan's own beach house a couple of miles away.

Over the months after her wedding, Maria and Olivia had spent many hours over Skype and email discussing the newly-weds' home design project. Maria had used almost all her suggestions and Olivia loved her even more because her best friend knew how she had welcomed and needed the distraction in those months following her recuperation.

She had refused to be a burden to anyone, especially her younger sister Lisa, or her friends during those months after her cancer treatments.

Now thinking of all the positives came easier to her. Helping others had been the best healing process for her. Most of the time she even forgot what she had gone through, as if it had happened to someone else.

She appreciated every moment as the gift that life was.

Every rewarding day was an adventure, and right now 'project Alexander the Geek' was proving very exciting, revealing and tempting.

By 5p.m. most evenings she was ready to shower at her hotel room and meet him either at the beach or at Aunt Jenny's back-yard lounge area. The space was private and the panoramic beach view was priceless.

They sat here now enjoying another cold glass of wine each.

"So what did you do then?" Olivia asked Alexander after he had told her about the fiasco which culminated with Sofia's break up.

"First I was angry and sad that I'd not seen how materialistic she was. Even my Papa," this was what he called his Greek biological father, "had been charmed by her. Then when my cousin Demetrius came and apologized for all that happened, I realized that although I'd believed I loved her, in reality I hadn't really... and that I had wasted months of my life when we'd been together."

"So have you gone out with anyone else since?" Olivia felt like a little girl playing at being a psychologist with nothing but curiosity and her need to help him driving her forward.

"No. I've been busy working. I see that look in your eyes, Olivia. I mean it." Alexander said and then his grin widened as if her frank stare was his undoing. He took off his glasses and pinched the bridge of his nose as if unaware he was doing this. "There weren't any girls I was interested in. And it's only been over a year."

"You're still counting. Are you sure you're not still in love with her? Because that wouldn't be fair on this new girl."

He put his glasses back on. "It's not a rebound situation. I'm sure of it."

"Okay, as long as you're not kidding yourself. Now, you said you're nearly ready, so tell me, why this girl?"

"When I saw her recently I just felt something I haven't felt in a long time." When he looked away from her, the way he said those words quashed any silly childish hope within her that he was still talking about *her*.

She was one lucky woman, whoever she was. Because Olivia suspected that Alexander was the one-woman type of man. Once he fell in love.

"So what's her name?" She asked through the slight obstruction in her throat.

For a moment Alexander was silent and then said, "Jessica."

"So let's do this. You'll call her tonight and ask her out, right?"

Despite his masculine girth, he shook his head like a little boy facing a hated injection. "Maybe first we can do some more role playing? It'll help me gain more confidence with making conversation."

"You said the same thing over the past week. I don't get it, Alexander, you're talking absolutely fine with me, and I'm a female… What's really holding you? What's the worst that can happen if you just ask her out? Rejection?"

Slowly he shook his head. "No. That I get to know her, that she gets to know me and she doesn't really see my true self."

"But surely everyone has that fear." Olivia said.

"Do *you*? When's the last time you went out with anyone?"

Her heart beat even stronger under his gaze. About to turn the conversation back to him, she remembered that these were his delay tactics, and perhaps he needed the role playing more than she thought. "I've been too busy. Interior design is my passion. I've had a couple of challenging years, but I've not been interested in dating." She kept it as honest as she could.

"Who's the last guy you got close to?" The split moment of something unrecognizable flitted through his bespectacled green eyes. Then his expression was unreadable as he listened intently.

"His name was Ryan and we went out for eight months over three years ago, and he left the country to pursue his photography career." She could not admit to Alexander that this happened the same week she had been about to go into hospital for breast cancer surgery. She had heard of men who could not handle this sort of thing, and was shocked at how little Ryan's departure had meant to her despite her predicament. Obviously he hadn't cared for her as much as she had thought. She couldn't really blame him to choose not to stay and deal with a girlfriend facing numerous challenges throughout the following year. Weeks of radiation after the two surgeries and…

Well, it was all behind her now and she had conquered cancer with her head held high.

Her sister Lisa and Maria had been all she had needed. She had learned to be as self-reliant as possible, because after all she was the older sister on whom Lisa depended.

"Are *you* counting?" Alexander stared deeper into her eyes.

Refusing to look away she shook her head. "No, it wasn't really his fault. We weren't compatible." Taking in another breath she added, "Aunt Jenny would say that all human beings are afraid to show themselves too soon, but I see it the other way.

You have to start as you mean to go on. It's better to find out if you're compatible sooner rather than after weeks or months of wasted energy, like you'd said about Sofia."

Alexander smiled, "You see? You're so wise. I was right to trust you."

Warmed by his words she nodded and asked, "So when do you plan to go forward with this?"

Alexander shrugged, broke eye contact with her and said, "I think I need another couple of days. There's a barbecue party this Saturday. I'll invite her to go with me, I suppose." His eyes seemed to ask her what she thought about that.

"Great." She pushed away the tightness in her chest. "Let's work with that. How would you like to role play?" As she said it out loud it sounded so silly. "Let me just ask... When you have a business meeting with a woman, how do you deal with her? Do you have any hesitations, or is it only a problem when you are attracted to the women?"

"It's different. I deal with the women in business the way I deal with all my work; professionally, respectfully and I don't mix business with *pleasure*." He said the word so softly, and catching his eyes move to her mouth again she was glad she wasn't holding her wine glass. Her heart skipped a few beats and then continued thumping erratically.

This time she knew it was not her imagination or wishful thinking.

She was confused. Because he was treating her with respect and not crossing the professional line, and yet those eyes said...

No, you're the buddy, and don't you forget it. He's hired your services, nothing more. And you don't want anything more.

Still thrown off by her gut instincts and what she read in those green eyes, she stood up, "Okay, so what will help you get more comfortable about approaching Jessica?"

He stood up too and scanned her face. "I think we can grab dinner right now and we can pretend we're on a real date."

"That's not necess—" She shut up. Always impulsive, she still had some ways to go to stop herself from answering too soon. She took a moment to think it through, admitted she was only afraid of forgetting that this was all part of role playing, and said, "Okay, I need half an hour, where would you like to meet?"

"Where do you suggest? Come to think of it I don't know your preferences."

She shook her head. "We'll have to work on you taking more initiative, Alexander. But this once I'll suggest the place."

~

*A*lex was enjoying their pseudo date.

Sitting opposite the lovely Olivia at the intimate dining table they were only feet away from the now dark sea, at the terrace of the busy yet relaxed South Beach Grill.

Of all the places in the world and all the high-class restaurants he had enjoyed over the years, this unassuming lovely hideout meant more to him than anything else. Because it had been one of his and Aunt Jenny's favorite haunts, and now he was here with Olivia.

Those memories of his excitement of their weeks together nearly a decade ago had not been exaggerated. His pulse still played that staccato drum beat. Every moment with her felt right.

The nagging voice inside his head reminded him about his underhandedness. He never lied to anyone, and was proud of his business integrity, and he wholeheartedly agreed with Olivia that it was best to be open and authentic from the start.

Now what the hell was he going to do?

He would enjoy her company and get to know her. He could tell her the truth tonight.

No time like the present.

If he didn't kiss her by the end of tonight, he would admit he was the biggest coward in the world and throw himself in the sea.

No nearly-thirty-year-old had a right to be this immature. Olivia was right, he ought to take more initiative!

But knowing that did nothing to help him.

Aunt Jenny would have firmly pushed him to just do it.

"Tell me more about your sister, Lisa." He speared a morsel of his grilled salmon with his fork and put it in his mouth. This was as good as he remembered at those lunches or dinners he had shared with Aunt Jenny spent laughing and enjoying watching the world go by.

Even though the sea was too dark right now, he could hear it and the salty scent intermingled with the delicious dishes being served around them. It all inspired momentary peace within him.

As Olivia talked about her younger sister it warmed him at how much she adored and worried about her. "She's in her second year of business school and once she finishes her exams she's got a summer job lined up at a law firm. She's so sophisticated, smart and beautiful."

So are you, he nearly blurted out, *you're even more lovely and giving than you were at eighteen.* But instead said, "She's lucky to have you for a sister." As they shared more about each other he relaxed and felt less like a fraud. He was not harming anyone, he was catching up with an old friend who was more than that. He had no idea how or when he ought to tell her that he didn't know any Jessica, and he had no plans to attend any barbecue party this Saturday.

"So you think she'll move back home?" He couldn't imagine life with just one sibling with no elders. He was so fortunate.

"I hope so, but she's twenty-two, and she has a good head on her shoulders so I'll support any life decision she makes." Her eyes were betraying her worry, and again he wished he knew the best way to earn her trust. Could spending time together prove to her who he really was?

But it's all based on a lie. His guilty conscience reminded him.

Why did Olivia take on all the responsibility, helping every stray soul? And why had he taken advantage of that wonderful trait? Again, he counted his blessings for both his adopted and biological families here and in Greece.

As if psychic or so attuned to Alex, Olivia said, "I'll bet you don't find our American food as palatable as what you're used to in Greece."

Alex smiled, "There's more salt in the food than what I'm now used to. And the fish there almost comes out literally from the sea onto your plate. Porto Heli is still a small busy port and yet it maintains its natural unspoiled beauty." He took out his cell phone and started searching for something.

His smile told Olivia that he was not checking business emails. As he offered it to her she saw gorgeous images of a quaint boating village, and the cobalt color of the sea was breathtaking.

"Wow." She couldn't help her wistfulness. "It's like a dream, it's so beautiful. Do you live with your father in Porto Heli?"

"No. I visit often, but I have my own place in Athens over-looking the Parthenon. Grey likes to stay with Papa whenever he comes in for business, too." Although she knew some of the facts about Grey's successful yacht manufacturing business from Maria and Gemma, she listened to Alexander's passion for his brothers and the business. "We both love our boats and sailing."

"Yes, I met Grey when I was taking one of Gemma's yoga classes. I love her gym. It's amazing."

Increasingly Olivia felt more at ease with her own body image, being inspired and spurred on by Gemma, who was such an inspiration on many levels. She loved watching her and Grey together. "And they're such a sweet and romantic couple."

"Yes, they are." Alexander sighed but then immediately concentrated on his phone. He leaned so close their heads almost touched as he swiped to another photo. "This is the *Asteria*."

The yacht appeared so enormous, she felt the instant separation between them. His expression told her that this boat was like a favorite pet. Something he enjoyed and took for granted. For her it symbolized the many differences between their backgrounds. She swallowed the lump in her throat and asked, "What does *Asteria* mean?"

He shrugged, "Something like Goddess of stars or dreams."

~

*A*lex enjoyed entertaining Olivia, and liked the way she listened so intently. He had never felt this at ease and totally happy with any other woman.

Every word he had said to Olivia about wanting to be proactive rather than reactive was true. He still couldn't justify having dated Sofia for all those months. No matter how he had tried he never felt relaxed around her like he did right now with Olivia. Like they had from the first day they had met.

When something had been missing, and despite his gut warning him that something was wrong in the way Sofia had acted, he had been sure it was because he was unrealistically expecting to feel like he had with his first love. He had been adamant that the past was a mirage and exaggerated with the passing of time.

Now he knew better. Only the real thing would do. He sat back and answered Olivia's questions and enjoyed every moment spent together.

He talked about his many cousins who had welcomed him with open arms all those years ago, sharing with him the amazing and delicious culture that was his biological legacy.

Perhaps because Sofia hadn't shown any interest in his past, he appreciated how curious Olivia was about his Greek background.

"When I decided to move to Porto Heli permanently Papa set me up in his business as an apprentice. For the first six months we kept it confidential that I was his son, and I went under my American name."

"You wanted to prove yourself."

He nodded, knowing she truly got him. Always had.

"I never knew you were adopted, you never told me about it back when—then."

"I was still working through things in my teens, and by the time we met I didn't see any reason to talk about it. I enjoyed my summers with my Greek family and then… life went on."

Even in the dim light he could see in her eyes that Olivia had questions. But that she wasn't going to voice them.

"I've never said anything about that time, but I want to apologize to you now."

"No need." Olivia said almost too fast. He saw how her shoulders rose a notch.

"You're a very special person, Olivia. Look at us now. Some girls wouldn't have even talked to me, but you're here helping me with my stupid…"

Say it, say it now. "Look, Olivia. I—"

She touched his hand on the table. "It's Okay, Alexander. I understand. Don't worry."

He took in a deep breath, forced himself to continue but no words would come out.

He exhaled slowly and consciously sat back into his chair.

"So tell me more about beautiful Greece." She invited with a smile.

"You'd love it and its people." He imagined her sitting around a table filled with fresh and delicious food they would share alongside his many cousins and other relatives.

He could see her laughing at their loud, over-the-top physical expressions of affection. He wondered if she would lose her inhibitions after a glass of ouzo and dance with him and the others under the grape-vine covered trellis hiding the big moon above them.

"My female cousins would envy your beauty." At her blush he hastened to add, "Your red hair and blue eyes."

"Greek women are the most gorgeous in the world with their black hair and amazing bone structure." Olivia said.

"And my male cousins would love to meet you." He smiled, he couldn't help it.

"So I'll let you know when I'm ready to date." She laughed.

Was that an innocent remark? He couldn't tell. He tried to keep his smile in place.

I don't want you to date anyone but me. Only me.

He focused on elaborating on life in Greece. He started telling her about his father, the eccentric uncles and aunts, until Olivia burst out laughing, grabbing her napkin to her mouth.

"You mean your aunt set you up with your cousin? Then what happened?"

"So Maria, the said short girl with a unibrow sat opposite me and kept staring at me. I smiled, making small conversation. And she then came to sit next to me." Alex tried not to laugh. "Okay, I thought, beginning to understand my aunt's winks and prods. And as I concentrated on what Maria was saying she flicked her big black braid my way, whatever she had at the base of it socked me in the eye and I fell back from the bench and hit my head on the concrete. I was okay, and thankfully when I awoke Maria had gone."

After a second's moment of silence Olivia burst out laughing. She held her tummy just under those luscious breasts, but Alex somehow managed to focus more on her laughing features than her delightful torso.

"They sound just like from the movie My Big Fat Greek Wedding. I thought Nia Vardalos had exaggerated it all in the name of art and comedy."

"No, that's actually pretty much what I'm used to these days, and I wouldn't change it for the world." He could hardly breathe at the pleasure he took in her laughter.

"I haven't heard your lovely laugh since…" He realized he had missed it so much and knew he would do anything and everything to extract that genuine unguarded happiness from within her.

As if needing to change the subject Olivia said, "I love sketching and painting from those images of Santorini, that incredible blue is unique. I've always gravitated back here to Wrightsville Beach, no matter where I am, but Santorini is one place that's always fascinated me."

He couldn't get enough of seeing that sparkle of inspiration in her blue eyes. "It's even more beautiful in real life. You must come and stay with me—or one of my many female cousins—and I'll show you around. We can sail there and I can fly us over the various islands on my helicopter. You'll love it."

And the guard came tumbling down as he watched her face.

No words were needed. He realized how ridiculous his invitation was.

She may as well have said, *Yes, that's what I'll do, I'll help you win over the girl of your dreams, and tag along while you sweep her off to paradise.*

He'd forgotten his own convoluted plan.

Go on, just tell her the truth right now. No time like the present, he reminded himself again.

But the coward stayed quiet.

"So tell me the truth…"

His heart nearly burst at her words. He stopped breathing until she waved a graceful hand towards the darkness and added, "Do you find all this…mundane?"

Letting his breath come out slowly he watched Olivia bite into a piece of shrimp and envied the fork for being so close to her delicious mouth.

He shifted in his seat. "Not at all, it was fun growing up here. I've always loved the beach and boating with Dad and Grey." Although the bond between all his siblings was extremely strong, he and Grey seemed more like twins in many ways. He smiled thinking of his brother being shot by Cupid's arrow, and how happy Grey and Gemma were. He just wished he could grow a little back bone and grab Olivia right now and kiss her and see if he was right about the spark between them was still there.

For the first time in a decade he felt it was possible for him to attain what all his brothers now had. They all had found love with their own soulmates.

Wasn't Olivia his?

Or was he was different from them?

He had to stop thinking like that. "And I have fond memories of this particular restaurant. I used to come here with Aunt Jenny until I left for good."

Her stricken expression made him wonder what was wrong.

"I didn't know that you knew Aunt Jenny so well."

"Yes, with our family summer home nearby, I started helping her out cutting grass, etc…when I was twelve."

"Oh, you never told me about that. And I never saw you here on those summers I stayed here with Maria. But of course, you spent them all in Greece."

"I have the best of both worlds, and believe me if we'd met when I was in my early teens you wouldn't have given me time of day." He smiled again as she shook her head. "On the other hand, you're too kind a person."

As she looked slightly jittery, her eye lashes fluttering as she looked away, he asked, "What do you do in your spare time, Olivia? Do you still play chess?"

She shook her head and at the sadness on her face he could have kicked himself. He remembered too late that she had played chess with her father. He had only discovered this past week from Maria that Olivia had lost both her parents three years ago. When he had asked for more information about her best friend and if she had any boyfriends, Maria had clammed up. "Talk to Olivia," Maria had dared him with that sparkle in her eyes.

"I'm sorry. I heard about your parents' passing. It must be so difficult for both of you."

She nodded. "Thanks."

He admired her tenacity as he listened. Olivia had lost them within months of each other; her mother had died from complications of pneumonia, and a few months later she lost her father. "He seemed to lose any purpose to go on living. I'd heard of that, but never witnessed it. He died from a heart attack." She then added, "But thank God Lisa and I have each other."

His heart went out to her, he wished he could touch her hand again, but knew it was inappropriate.

He wanted to bring back that glint in her large blue eyes, "What about your painting? Do you have time for that? You were excellent from what I remember."

"Yes, it's been my savior." Suddenly she stopped. The adorable blush blossomed over her features as she added, "I find painting very cathartic, healing and relaxing." Olivia studied him and asked, "What about you? You still play tennis and squash?"

He nodded, glad she remembered. "I now also enjoy a game of golf."

Her shoulders came down a little, as she smiled, "Is it true what they say, that many business transactions get done on the golf course?"

"Yes." The golf resorts he frequented were part of the many he owned, which he had developed over the past few years. The international locations of the Luxe Clubs were good for the bottom line and his extensive business portfolio.

As they shared a decadent piece of chocolate cake he couldn't help staring and enjoying Olivia's patent pleasure of her every bite.

He couldn't hide his grin as she licked her lower lip and said, "Don't look at me like that. Certain things are just worth it. Without my chocolate cake and a good bowl of spaghetti bolognaise—life's not worth living."

He chuckled and said, "A woman after my own heart. My mother would agree with you, too."

He wished he could tell Olivia how he saw her, how much he wanted to touch her, and that to him she was perfect the way she was. But he refrained from saying anything personal knowing she would not appreciate him stepping over the professional boundaries she had set.

Neither would she believe that his interest in her was genuine.

After all he was supposed to be getting ready to woo 'Jessica'.

But from deep within him a voice goaded him to go ahead, move even closer to her and kiss her.

Their kiss could reignite their special connection. But what if it backfired on him and instead resulted in a swift end to their association?

No, he sat immobile, staring at her as the moments of opportunity fizzled and disappeared.

Fool, *Touvlo!* The Greek word described him perfectly. The coward that he was, he *was* as thick as a brick.

"So in preparation for the party we should hit the mall first thing tomorrow, if you like. That way if I'm delayed on site later you'll still be ready for Saturday. Are you ready to call Jessica tonight?"

He shrugged then nodded slowly. He felt like a heel, knowing that he could organize the so-called makeover by himself. She was generous to a fault. "I'll try. Thanks, Olivia." He couldn't meet her eyes. He adjusted his glasses slightly back on the bridge of his nose.

From little white lies, big honking lies can grow.

*A*lexander must have felt embarrassed last night at dinner to be reminded about the makeover. But Olivia took her responsibilities seriously and it was for a good cause.

Yes, remind yourself that, Olivia!

After specific instructions to the designer hair stylist about how to trim Alexander's hair and beard, she sat down to check her many messages. She tried not to laugh at Alexander's wary expression as he stared at his reflection as the stylist held his scissors inches from his dark head. She couldn't wait to see him in a suit and a dress shirt at their next stop. How could he be as successful as he obviously was from what she had seen and heard about him, when he dressed so casually compared to his other brothers? Or was he one of those men who disliked constrictive ties and wore designer suits only for business?

He was here visiting family and relaxing, after all. When she had asked him last week about his work attire, he had merely confirmed that he was ready for a new, updated look. That was all he would say and she had left it there.

If she had spare money she would have a closet full of gorgeous outfits and shoes. Sure, she preferred comfortable and flowing outfits, but she now admitted that adopting her so-called bohemian style in decor and fashion from the gregarious Aunt Jenny were partly an excuse.

When she looked up she had to search for Alexander. Had he been moved? Focusing, she saw a slimmer man with familiar striking eyes connect with hers in the mirror.

Alexander?

How could the stylist have transformed him in less than half an hour?

She stared at the reflection until her Cinderfella swiveled in his chair to face her. "So, do I pass the test?" As he smirked and put his glasses back on, his designer beard now accentuated his bone structure, delicious mouth and that strong jaw line. His haircut and beard trim highlighted the shape of his well-formed skull, his proud Greek nose, and his eyes appeared even greener and more astute.

And dangerously sexy.

She inhaled realizing she had stopped breathing momentarily. "Yes, absolutely." Her voice seemed strange. She stood up and turned away from him. "Let's go. Next stop, suit and accessories."

An hour later they left the mall with Alexander's divine Armani suit and the rest of the paraphernalia. Olivia had to get back to the beach house not because she was needed there, but because she was too shaken up by seeing the newly outfitted Alexander.

Something within her boiled dangerously. Why would he hide behind the dark, loose-fitting clothes?

That wasn't really what bugged her.

She was livid with her own reaction and the strong pull towards him. In her opinion all his brothers were great looking but from what she had heard about and seen for herself from Sloan and Grey, all the siblings were the whole package; wonderful human beings and great sons and husbands.

Maria and Gemma gave Olivia hope that real 'happy-everafters' existed outside fairy-tales. That there were trustworthy and loving guys out there.

Yes, his brothers were incredible men, but Alexander's modesty made Olivia want to scream. He was the perfect specimen of masculinity and sensitivity and she constantly wanted to blurt out, "You shouldn't pretend or try to be something you're not. Don't do anything you don't want to in order to attract some girl. Be yourself and she should accept you just the way you are."

Boy, oh boy, look at how he cleaned up! Before she cried like a fanatic fan facing her Hollywood idol, or before she grabbed him, planted a hungry kiss on his sensuous lips, and jumped his bones in the middle of the high street, she resolved to escape into her work.

As they reached her car Alexander said, "I really appreciate your help. I have a favor to ask you."

He looked sheepish, but she was too distracted by his gorgeous thick black lashes, now that his eyebrows had also been tamed.

"Yes, what is it?" at her rushed words she stopped. *Calmly, Olivia!* In a more civil voice she said, "I'm at your service." And smiled.

"There's a social function tonight. Would you please join me?"

Before she could refuse she counted to five and then asked, "What kind of do is it? What do I wear?"

"It's formal, but we don't need to stay for long."

Having packed solely for work and the beach, she supposed raiding Maria's wardrobe was in order. She nodded.

She saw his relief and gratitude in that smile, "I'll pick you up at eight at the hotel?" For someone who could have anything or any beauty he desired his self-consciousness amazed her. Or perhaps it was his sensitive and shy nature.

Had Sofia DeLongi screwed up his self-esteem to such an extent?

After having spent many hours together over the past ten

days she understood that to Alexander women and relationships were still out of his comfort zone. Kudos to him for trying to deal with it.

~

*A*lex was stunned and couldn't help staring at Olivia. Her little black dress showed off her delectable curves and she looked even more feminine. And how could she have become even sexier?

But she appeared a little self-conscious in it and in the black high heels that accentuated her lovely ankles and her long, shapely legs.

Tonight, she seemed less distracted about her work, having hurried back to the beach house earlier today.

He wished she would look into his eyes. Because he wanted to read her thoughts and couldn't.

Was she angry with him for some reason?

Ask her about it.

As he took in a breath about to forge into his confession, he was welcomed by the organizer of the charity gala. "I'm so glad you changed your mind, Mr. Anderson. It means more than you can imagine having you present to accept the award."

Olivia's eyes questioned him as they were ushered to the front of the large crowded hall to a beautifully laid table. The high glittering chandeliers above them caught the mirror centre pieces. All eyes from the other tables followed Olivia and Alex until he helped her into her seat and sat next to her. Somehow despite feeling more exposed because of his new frameless glasses, Olivia's presence helped him.

"You really don't like being out in public, do you?" Olivia still sounded annoyed. "When did the soiree start?"

"Not that long ago." He shrugged and heard the MC address the audience, "It's a genuine privilege to have our own founder and CEO of "Children's Better World" organization here with us tonight. Although he likes to work behind the scenes I'm honored to invite him to please come up and accept the CBW Excellence Award. Mr. Alexander Anderson."

With the loud applause erupting around him, Alex strode up to the podium.

"Thank you so much everyone. Please sit," he said, uncomfortable and yet aware that they just wanted to show their appreciation for all the good the charity organization was able to achieve. "Ever since I was little, a special, kind lady taught me to see things from other people's perspectives and never judge people by the way they dress, what they drive or by their backgrounds." His eyes naturally sought out Olivia's face in the crowd. "Mrs. Jennifer Ellis always said that the best way of making a difference is to start small, within yourself. I was one of the few children who were lucky to have two big families who have loved and accepted me just the way I am. I grew up with four incredible brothers and many cousins here and in Greece. Our parents brought us up to be aware of how privileged we were to live in a peaceful country with so much choice all around us. Traveling around the world over the past few years, my mission strengthened further to ensure we can all help the many children from war-torn cities and third-world countries where we can bring a little joy, quench their thirst, feed their bellies, heal their bodies and their souls. And most importantly find them new homes and families to show them love, and if we can, replace—if not erase—some of their traumatic memories."

~

$\mathcal{A}$lexander stopped and scanned the large room with the smiling and enthralled faces, and Olivia had never been prouder of anyone if her life. She was learning so much about him just from his words. His drive and passion from the heart made her love him even more.

What? Where did that spring from?

She was not in love with him....

Yet she felt shaken as she focused on the man at the podium. This was not love, but mere hero worship. She was enjoying the familiar feeling of being with her first teenage crush. And she had to stop revisiting her romantic teen years, pretending they were actually seeing each other.

He *was* one heck of a sophisticated man now, despite his shyness. Perhaps she was appreciating how lucky she had been to have shared her first sexual experience with such a special man.

But they were different people now. They had never actually belonged in the same orbit.

Collecting herself Olivia realized that Alexander's shyness was nowhere to be seen, because of his commitment to this amazing cause, she supposed. She now understood that it was only one of many other good causes he had initiated. It appeared Aunt Jenny had been a major influence in his life, too.

Had the romantic Aunt Jenny played cupid nearly a decade ago by sending Alexander to help with the gala so they would meet each other?

As the huge screen behind Alexander flashed with images of him surrounded by dark-skinned children in a dusty, poor village, clad in a khaki shirt sleeves rolled up to his elbows, his compassionate eyes and smile tugged at her heart. Olivia's respect for him escalated. He was a true philanthropist.

Staring at Alexander, Olivia wondered what other surprises and secrets he held.

CHAPTER 7

Respecting his reticence to discuss his childhood Olivia had not asked anything about it. Therefore, she had appreciated it when he had opened up about it as they strolled by the shore last night. "Grey's only ten months older than I, and although we are very close and love each other, during my teens it frustrated me how over protective they all were, never really taking me seriously. Some of the best times were those hours spent on whichever boats Dad and Grey were working on. I got the boating bug from them both." Then he had smiled and added, "Mom has always treated me like one of her own, I've always taken it for granted, but I admire her as I grow older and see what she's like with Tyler and baby Jordan and the neighborhood kids. I just wish she'd stop pushing me to—" When he'd stared at Olivia she waited and he added, "Mom always tells me there's more to life than work."

Olivia had wished she could read his mind at that moment. Had he been pressured to also settle down with the right girl? Was Jessica his one and only? Or was he hoping that she was and feared rejection so much?

Even now as Olivia listened to Alexander addressing the

waiting audience, filled with joy at his accomplishments and his generous charitable heart, the thought of another woman capturing his interest triggered such pain inside that she had to push it away.

"I'm glad that with all your help and commitment this organization can continue helping so many needy children and families." Then he called out some people's names and asked them to stand up. He had no list in front of him.

One after another, over a dozen men and women stood, surrounded by loud applause.

She fought tears of pride as Alexander added, "You are all the reason CBW is growing from strength to strength and we can all continue changing the world one city, one orphanage, one child at a time. Thank you from the bottom of my heart. Keep up the great work." He seemed to have almost forgotten what he was holding. Now he raised the heavy crystal rectangular award on its black base and smiled, "And thanks for this."

As Alexander descended the few steps back towards her she stared at him and tried to form some words. Instead she touched his hand and before she thought about what she was doing she pressed her lips against his.

～

*W*as Alex dreaming? Was Olivia Moore kissing him? He refused to wake up, ever! As he was about to deepen the kiss Olivia moved away with an expression that told him she had acted on impulse and regretted it.

"The problem with you seems that you're too modest. You should stop hiding the real you and transfer that confidence," she nodded towards the podium, "into your personal, romantic life." Was she trying to compose herself? He heard the breathy way she had said that, as if determined to sound professional. But she could not hide the flush of pleasure she had obviously shared during the too-short few seconds of their kiss.

He was growing wings of hope. Maybe she felt more for him than merely as a Samaritan for a doofus client.

"The food's good, you want to stay awhile?" Perhaps he could muster up some courage to dance with her. She would do it in the name of her 'responsibility' to help him.

She nodded. A few minutes later she said, "You obviously have quite a lot of public speaking experience and a huge following." Her eyes sparkled with respect. "I had no idea you've traveled so extensively. And now I understand that perhaps your earlier bushy beard was not your usual style. I didn't know you'd just returned from Kenya a few weeks ago. You do incredible work. I'm beginning to wonder if you really need my help, and if you really are that shy in your personal life."

This is your perfect opportunity. Alex wanted was to tell her the truth about everything: Why he was in town, why he had wanted her 'help' and about the non-existent Jessica.

The woman I want to woo is you! All I want is you, Olivia, just the way you are. Perfect.

But his throat closed up yet again and he shook inside. Obviously misunderstanding his reaction, the sensitive Olivia touched Alex's hand again and said, "Don't worry, I'm here. You'll do just fine tomorrow. Just take some of the energy and drive you had up there," Olivia pointed to the podium, "and you'll sweep Jessica off her feet."

What was that fleeting emotion he saw within her expressive eyes?

Don't let your wishful thinking play tricks on you. He reminded himself.

As they enjoyed the delicious menu, the pleasure of having her in his arms as they danced was marred by his cowardice.

Frustration bristled within him, becoming increasingly impatient with himself as the heat and the rightness of being together fanned his hunger for her. He wanted to kiss Olivia and hold her tighter instead of merely dancing with her. He wanted to explore every curve and crevice of her gorgeous body, and quench the desire within him. To prove with action—and the right words, damn it—that he had grown up and was experienced in love and love-making.

And to be honest with her.

What would it take to grow a backbone? Why could he face an army of opposition and controversy in his business deals, turn over a new leaf after breaking up with Sofia, and yet clam up in front of the soft, generous Olivia?

And what if he was misreading her emotions? *Be positive, damn it.*

What if by some miracle his purging admission was met by her reciprocating his feelings? What if she also felt their physical attraction and emotional synchronicity?

But he was not the purging type. Despite having meant every word about being fortunate in his family life, he now felt even more trapped within his lie. Olivia was a genuine person who deserved the truth.

What could he do or say now and not risk losing Olivia's trust again?

As he maneuvered her across the dance floor and the music changed to a slower romantic ballad Alex took in a deep breath and said softly in her ear, "I don't think there will ever be the right time to discuss what happened and why I left all those years ago, but—" As she pulled slightly away to look into his eyes he shook his head, "Please, Olivia, I need to say this." As his gentle fingers invited her head to rest on his shoulder he felt better not seeing those expressive eyes as he continued, "I was a fool and I needed to tell you that." When again she shifted he said, "Please let me finish. I ran because I felt so much so soon and I don't think I was ready for any of it. I justified everything over the next months as I got into my new life and work in Athens, but I just couldn't forget you."

She looked into his eyes and after a few long moments she shook her head slowly. "We're here now, and are having such a lovely evening why rehash the past which we cannot change?"

The coward in him took the easy way out yet again.

CHAPTER 8

As Alexander drove her back to her hotel, Olivia was giddy from the night's incredibly romantic atmosphere, and dizzy from what she was uncovering about the enigmatic, powerful man.

How good that momentary kiss had felt.

She was still swooning from all that time in his arms as he held and led her like a professional dancer. There was such a certainty and sense of purpose about him that was so contradictory to his obvious shyness.

Once again, she wondered about how could she really help him? And could she go through with watching him win over another girl?

And wishing she was from his world could never make it so.

When she heard him speak at the charity event with such conviction from his heart she remembered why she had been so attracted to him in her teens. It had been so much more than merely a first sexual experience with someone she had trusted and desired...And believed she loved.

Until he had left without a word of goodbye. Even Aunt

Jenny's explanations and placations of his need to grow up had not helped one bit.

Leave the past where it belongs.

As Alexander parked outside the hotel and walked her to her door she was too aware of the virile man she was really seeing properly for the first time. Like a magnet she felt pulled towards him, but blamed the earlier couple of glasses of the excellent wine. There was no doubt from his hungry glances that the sparks between them were driving him crazy too. She had wanted to continue pretending there was no Jessica in his heart.

When he had started talking about their past she had been so tempted to tell him that all was forgiven that she stopped him from delving further into his reasons.

He had seemed so disappointed as if he had needed to confess, but what was the difference now? Neither could bring back that decade.

And, she reminded herself, he was doing everything she had suggested so far in order to win over some other girl.

"Goodnight, Alexander, and thanks for a nice evening. You're ready for tomorrow. G-good luck." With the key card poised she turned away from the frank disappointment on his face.

She had to escape his sexual magnetism, and from those eyes which seemed to beckon her to him from behind his new frame-less glasses.

When his muscular arms pulled her back to face him and he kissed her, it felt strangely natural. She melted into him and felt positively dainty within his large grasp.

Dizziness overcame her at his determination and demanding mouth. She feared she would lose her balance if he let her go. But that seemed the last thing on his mind as he explored her mouth, his eyes shut as if he was in agony.

Despite having been kissed by a few other men since her teens this was the feeling she had been waiting for. The perfect fit of their mouths and the instant fire igniting within her belly.

"Oh, God, Olivia," he ground out the words against her lips as if he needed her to save him. "It feels so right, so absolutely perfect, just like I remember it." He opened his eyes and she tried to pull back against her door.

The fire within his green eyes was no longer that of a twenty-year-old guy, but of a determined, intense, hot-blooded man.

As his body imprisoned her against the door, she saw no shyness or hesitation, just desire and need. And she was sure that her own eyes betrayed how much she wanted him too.

But he wouldn't let her break their eye contact. "Please let me in, I have to talk to you. I want you, Olivia. I need you." He held her face tenderly between his large hands. His heart thumped against her chest, and her breasts tingled. Goosebumps overtook her too warm body and her nipples pebbled against him.

Like a desperate man who knew the same torment, his gentle hands explored the nape of her neck, her hair, lowering to her arms and under her breasts. She shuddered and couldn't stop her arms from winding around his corded neck.

Inhaling hurt her throat and she felt light headed from his scent.

His expert thumbs teasing her nipples made her groan.

Dizzy, she held on to him and then he kissed her so deeply, so thoroughly that she felt tears threaten to surface.

It was nostalgic, it was joyous, it was perfect.

How many years had she relived these kisses, waking in the middle of the night, alone? Missing him, wondering if her memories had merely gathered undeserving legendary status.

These strong arms and gentle fingers held and caressed her slowly and so tenderly, reawakening those deep, hungry, forgotten places within herself. As he lowered his warm mouth to her left breast and aroused the other with slow fingers she melted into his intensity and revelled at his brisling cheek against the exposed skin of her neck and bosom.

When he ground his manhood against her she heard another

guttural sound. It was her own. She needed him right now, all the way, consequences and reality be damned.

Was she out of her mind? Definitely.

"No, Alexander." Breathless and shaking, she opened her eyes, tried and failed to pull away from him. Fear and frustration helped her gain a semblance of strength to force her trembling palms against his bulk and hiss, "Let go of me."

She hated having to be strong for them both even if she was no match for his physical strength. To Alexander this was lust, and she reminded herself that he had hired her to help him win over his dream woman, whom he was meeting tomorrow.

"So you think that just because you tried to apologize about the past that you can…" She took another deep breath and let it out. "That's not part of the service." She deliberately said it firmly, almost coldly. Reminding herself too.

His fingers loosened around her, and he slowly pulled away from her inch by inch. Leaving unwelcome cold behind where desire and want had been seconds earlier. He frowned and the hurt in his eyes darkened their green depths. But she resolved to stand her ground despite her own gnawing hunger deep inside her abdomen.

She was flesh and blood after all, with sexual needs of her own, damn him.

"Please listen to me, Olivia, I'm so sorry, I need to tell you something. Now." He said it urgently, but she was losing her thread of thought.

She caught him starting at her mouth again and knew she had to stop this escalating madness before they both regretted it.

"Let me go, Alexander. Go home, have a cold shower, a large strong coffee, whatever…And think hard about what you really want."

When she pushed at him again, he left her personal space. Becoming aware of the cold air against her upper chest, she realized the straps of her dress were down around her forearms, and her left breast was bare. Sucking in a gasp, mortified, she turned away while pulling up the straps.

She glanced at him over her shoulder. "You were gung ho about wanting Jessica and here you are . . . seducing me. Go before I lose all respect for you. In fact, I can't believe that I fell for all this."

She took in a deep breath and let it go, and refused to meet his stare. "I don't want your money or to see you again. Just leave. Now." With every word Olivia's voice constricted within her throat.

Had she overtly led him on? Had he felt her vulnerability and as a red-blooded man hadn't been able to resist the easy pickings?

Tears threatened again, about to leave her at the mercy of this man who still had so much power over her. She craved his touch, wanted him so badly, she felt ashamed.

Then she fumbled with her card key, unlocked the door and rushed in without looking back.

Locking it, her fevered and frustrated body sank to the floor, and her tears gushed out now that the door was safely between them.

How could she have forgotten everything but the pleasure of Alexander's kisses, like she had years ago?

Yes, she was disgusted and disappointed with his actions, but deeper than that she could never admit to him the other under-lying fact. How would Alexander react—what would he have said —if it had been her right breast that had been bared last night? Would he accept her if he discovered about her brush with cancer?

Or run…

After Ryan's rejection she wouldn't let anyone know what she had gone through. She didn't want their pity, or to lose anyone, especially someone like this incredible handsome man. Who was interested in someone else; someone who was probably perfect in every way.

CHAPTER 9

Touvlo! Alex was one hell of an idiot! Hadn't he known how Olivia would see his actions as absolutely animal-istic and crude?

If he'd plucked up some damned courage, admitted to her that she was the one he wanted then the kiss would have been the perfect beginning to their love story.

Instead he'd screwed up, royally.

Now he had lost her trust absolutely, and he was supposed to have matured somewhat over the past decade. How could she know that he had never experienced this sort of unleashed phys-ical and emotional closeness and liberation with anyone? All these years he had attributed their first time together having been special because of their sexual connection. That it was their shared bond, losing their virginities together.

Only years later after having left for Greece had he realized that their union had been packed with so much more than two youths in love with the idea of love. In his mid twenties, always a slow bloomer in the arena of love and romance, he had become certain that their connection was rare and not to be taken for granted. He had avoided any chance of bumping into Olivia whenever he had visited Wrightsville Beach. Afraid of his own feelings, and more importantly, not wanting to face how much he had hurt her. When he had not seen her at Sloan and Maria's wedding, Alex had been more disappointed than he had anticipated.

Now, he so wanted to treat her the way Olivia deserved to be treated. She was unique and special to him and always would be. He wanted to woo her, to spend time getting to know each other.

Olivia gave him that sense of belonging that he only ever felt with his family. With the gregarious and generous Olivia he felt he could do no wrong.

As he dragged his feet through the pathway to the shore he looked over the darkness, listened to the deep ocean night sounds and closed his eyes.

Their kiss had unleashed the memories of their first time together and he couldn't—didn't want to—resist all those emotions from flooding over him.

~

They were both equally as committed to the Gala and here they were, one night before the big event, excited and almost giddy with accomplishment.

"Let me help you with those." Alex took the tall pile of the pristine pressed white napkins from Olivia's grasp, and as his hands touched hers something happened.

He knew she felt it too because she pulled back from him so quickly some of the top napkins got dislodged and floated to the floor beside them. But neither seemed to care. He let the rest follow so nothing stood between them.

Her long eyelashes fluttered around her shocked blue eyes, her cheeks grew that betraying pink and made him lose the grip over the remaining load of the heavenly scented fresh linens.

As if propelled by a power stronger than himself he stared at

Olivia's dilating pupils and drew slightly closer into her. She didn't move, just stared up at him, biting her lower lip. Feeling somewhat lightheaded and hungry he took in a steadying breath. The warm, fresh linen closet in the depths of the Hyatt hotel surrounded them both, cocooning them in the eerie silence.

Soft romantic music harmonized with the whooshing in his ears as he took a tentative step closer to Olivia until she craned her neck even more.

She pulled back slightly until shelves laden with white bed sheets and towels stopped her. But the eyes held no apprehension or hesitation as he neared her.

They were both on the same wavelength, yet again. He felt a smile tug at his mouth, he couldn't help it. Instead of fear and shyness he felt he was home.

As he slowly raised his hands and then his arms around her waiting for her to stop him or at least react, he couldn't help scan her face, her lips and the way her upper chest rose and fell.

As he lowered his mouth to hers he felt her sweet breath and heard her soft gasp. She leaned her head back and her large eyes seemed to flicker, her long dark eyelashes slowly closing.

Was she going to faint? Or did she want him to kiss her as much as he needed to finally taste her lips.

It's now or never.

He leaned in and finally they were kissing. He couldn't close his eyes he was so afraid that he was dreaming again. He couldn't risk waking up if he was. Not this time.

It was magical despite their location. It was perfect and unforgettable.

～

*A*s Alex brought himself back to the present he realized his vision was blurred due to his tears.

He had accepted defeat as a twenty-year-old.

Now he could not! Olivia was too important to him, always had been.

He had to do something. But he had to wait until morning.

After a sleepless night of drinking coffee while walking on the beach, Alex returned to Olivia's hotel room door. He had some damage control to take care of with no more procrastination. He needed Olivia's trust and nothing short of having her in his life would suffice. He had to win her completely. To prove to her that he deserved her and that he could make her happy.

Outside her hotel room he was about to knock when the door flung open and Olivia gave a short, sharp shriek. "What the h-heck? What are you doing here? It's 7am." She held her hand to her chest.

He saw that she was ready for her run but this was important.

"I'm sorry. This won't take long. May I please come in?" At her suspicious expression, with her hands on her upper hips, he added, "I promise to behave."

He would keep his promise even though all he wanted was to take her into his arms, hold her tight, kiss her and tell her that he would do anything for her. That it would all work out once he explained himself, and finally admitted how he really felt about her.

She retreated into her room and he followed her in. "I'm listening, Alexander." She stepped back from him.

He stood where he was and sighed. This was going to be difficult, and risky. "I don't regret what happened last night. It brought back all sorts of wonderful memories of us... No, hear me out, and then I'll leave you alone."

Blushing, she closed her mouth.

Then he said, "I've tried to tell you something that you won't be happy with. I'm so sorry, but I'm not interested in anyone else but you."

"What do you mean? You changed your mind about Jessica?

That's a great turnaround." She frowned, like he was a fickle immature guy who changed his mind all the time.

"I was never interested in any Jessica. I came to town to tie up some loose ends for . . . family, and I met you on the beach. Since then all I wanted was a chance to get to know you. There's no Jessica, or any other girl, in fact. Just you." At the tightness of her full lips he added, "I'm sorry, I went about this all wrong. It was childish, but that's the truth."

"So you didn't need my so-called help and you offered to pay me all that money? Are you crazy?" Her voice rose and she took a step towards him with the fire in her eyes. She blinked again and continued to stare.

He felt like a complete fool that he was. "What can I tell you? I'm an idiot." He tried to lighten the mood, but it seemed to incite her further. Was she going to smack him upside the head?

He couldn't blame her.

"Please just leave me alone." She pushed past him and left the room. "We revisited the past which we should have left behind and now just let's move on.

He followed her down the hall, "Olivia, I've apologized—"

She turned for a moment and said, "I know you'll soon return to Greece, but over the next couple of weeks please just let me do my work. And I'd appreciate it if when our paths cross in the future just let's be civil with each other. In the meantime it's obvious to me you still need to grow up."

Her open disappointment made him wonder why he had come up with such a pathetic, convoluted plan when all Olivia needed was simple honesty. Now she didn't even want to talk to him.

Touvlo! He uttered under his breath as he watched her disappear out of his life. His Papa father would have probably called him *thick as a brick* as well as a *stubborn mule in Greek*.

CHAPTER 10

"It's very kind of you to offer to babysit Jordan." His sister-in-law Gemma kissed his cheek. "And very nice wardrobe and designer stubble you've got there." She smiled. "Trying to impress someone?"

He could see from Gemma's laughing blue eyes that she saw right through his plan.

"Maybe. And what uncle wouldn't want to spend some quality time with one of his very favorite nephews in the whole wide world?" Alex cooed at the cherubic, blond seven-month-old Jordan his brother Grey unloaded into his waiting arms.

"As his Godfather and my youngest brother, you'd better look after him, Xander." Grey grinned in his good natured way and added, "At least all that experience with your gazillion Greek cousins gives us a free babysitter while you're in town. Okay, we're off. So, no girls allowed, unless they're pretty."

Grey's wife jabbed her husband playfully in the ribs and said, "You have our numbers and they're also on the fridge, and Jordan won't need anything after his seven-thirty bottle."

"I know, you said that already." Alex pushed his brother towards the door.

As Gemma followed her husband, still smiling, she said, "I also left some turkey sandwiches enough for two with plenty of your favorite kale, spinach and blue cheese salad, with extra fig and balsamic dressing on the side."

Was Gemma trying to delay leaving just to play on his nerves? "Great, thanks. Just go."

Now for the "Grow up and earn Olivia's trust" mission. He prayed that Olivia wouldn't see through his ruse again. The nagging voice at the back of his head kept reminding him that this could backfire—again.

~

"What do you mean you're in trouble? Why did you agree to babysit Jordan if you don't know what you're doing?" Olivia's heart was palpitating, shocked at Alexander's sheepish admission over the phone. "I'm too busy, I'm sorry. Just call your mother and she'll be right there."

"No," Alexander said urgently. "I don't want anyone to know, I'll never hear the end of it. They'll laugh and taunt me."

"Serves you right if they do, but don't be ridiculous—"

"Please Olivia," He said urgently.

"Call Maria if you don't want Grey to know about—"

"Olivia, I know you're still upset with me, but I need your help. Only yours. Just for a short while until Jordan falls asleep." He begged her.

She sighed, frustration and something else warred within her. "I'll be there in ten minutes." Yet the anticipation of seeing the insufferable man grew within her.

So much for staying away from him!

As she entered Gemma's and Grey's lovely new beach home she scanned the area and saw nothing out of the ordinary. Then Alexander strode towards her with the chubby, delicious seven-month-old Jordan in his strong arms. The chubby baby seemed in good spirits as usual. But Alexander appeared relieved to see her. "You're a life saver, Olivia! Thank you for coming. We have to feed him and change his diaper."

"We?" She rolled her eyes and then gave the brightest smile to the baby. "Only ignorant or chauvinist men think that all females are born with the nurturing gene. Don't they, Jordan?" She wanted to reach for the adorable dimple-cheeked baby and play peek-a-boo with him, but wouldn't make it too easy on the man child who had got himself into this mess.

She peeked sideways at the said handsome fool who now looked like a buff movie star with his toned muscles clearly outlined through the beautiful pale blue dress shirt and dark hip-hugging pants, and asked, "What makes you think I know how to look after a baby?"

"Sorry, my bad. But I quickly searched it online and I think I can manage the diaper but I couldn't trust myself not to pinch his baby skin."

She cringed away and then reached for Jordan, who readily obliged by hugging her as she held him. As he nuzzled his blond head into her throat his soft fine hair tickled her. She inhaled his talcum fresh baby smell. "Let's do it together, shall we?"

As they cleaned up Jordan's wet diaper, Olivia said, "Thank goodness it's not number two, you'd have been on your own then. Sorry, baby, you know I love you but there's a limit to what I'll do even for you." She tickled his tummy and resisted grabbing his toes and kissing them. "You're so adorable I want to eat your tootsies," she cooed. But seeing Alexander staring at her with that strange almost star-struck expression she cleared her throat. "Right, so let's see how we can heat that milk bottle and feed him before he starts to get irritable."

"You see, you *are* a natural." Alexander grinned at her and she was tempted once again to smack the Greek Adonis across that face.

She knew her frustration was also due to her distraction by

his physique. She wished he would revert to wearing those over-size clothes so she wouldn't be tempted to stare at his pecs and abs and remember how they felt as they had danced. . . .

"You say that again and I'll whack you and tell your family I gave you the black eye."

This seemed to increase his amusement which he obviously tried to control—unsuccessfully.

He raised his hands as if offering a truce, and then said, "I'd like you to try. See how fast you are." But his frank gaze was challenging her to a different kind of duel.

Balling her fists, she stopped herself from getting closer to him.

"Don't tempt me." She tried to even her breathing and then she smiled, "Or I can just leave."

That erased his smug gorgeous smirk. "No fair." He grumbled like an overgrown, naughty boy, reminding Olivia of Tyler, when the two-year-old accidently knocked over his toy trains off their tracks.

"You just can't help it, you're a natural chauvinist. I'm here to make sure Jordan is safe. So, how about you don't speak at all?"

Again she saw the twitch at the corners of those lips as he obviously tried to erase his smirk.

She gently laid Jordan in his uncle's arms and exited the nursery. She had to make sure to leave as much physical space as possible between the man who had haunted her every waking and sleeping moment of the last few days. No matter how busy she was at the beach house her wayward mind veered back to how she had felt in his arms against her hotel door....

Stop that and concentrate on feeding baby Jordan. And then get the heck out....

Leaving the nursery, she practiced her calming deep breathing exercises. In the kitchen she heated a saucepan of water then dunked Jordan's bottle in it, and kept checking its temperature. Then like she had seen in movies, she shook a couple of the drops of milk on her inner wrist and nodded.

Hearing Alexander behind her she swiveled round and offered Jordan's bottle to the uncle. "Here you go. Now you sit and feed Jordan and then don't forget to burp him. That's important."

He smiled and raised an eyebrow, "You're really something, you know that? Is there anything that you can't do?"

So much for expecting obedience and silence. It was like demanding the sun shouldn't shine.

"Lots and lots of things." She nearly said, *including resisting you, you big gorilla,* but instead added, "No flattery needed. You don't need me anymore. And I have to go."

"Oh, no." Alexander said urgently and at Jordan's surprised stare he smiled and said softly, "We'd very much like your company while we watch anything you choose on the TV. Even a chick flick." His eagerness—or was it his fear of being left alone with Jordan—was laughable, if not cute.

"Very magnanimous of you, but I have to go."

"Olivia, I need you—I mean we need supervision. I'll never forgive myself if I don't burp him properly. Give me a start-up company with hundreds of unhappy employees and I'll get it all into shape. But a baby?" He widened his eyes just for comic effect, she was sure.

How could she still find him witty and humorous?

"I don't believe you, and why on earth did you agree to babysit in the first place?" She shook her head, confused. "I'd have thought Grey would have known you better than to trust you with his only offspring."

"It seemed like a good idea at the time?" He didn't seem sure about this.

"I still don't believe you, but for Jordan's sake, I'll stay until he's finished his bottle." She tried not to grin at his patent relief.

His smile tempted her so badly to snuggle into those big

strong arms and pretend the blond baby was their own. "You're my hero, Olivia."

And you were mine all those years ago. But she clamped her lips shut and grabbed the remote control fully intending to make Alexander suffer through the sappiest romantic movie she could find.

An hour later well into the film, *The Notebook*, Olivia realized her big mistake. What had she been thinking? Her silly, impulsive revenge plan backfired, as now she could not stop the movie without looking like coward.

"Why is it taking Jordan such a long time?" She swiveled her head to see Jordan's cherubic face in the crook of Alexander's arm, and saw him sleeping and not suckling on the teat of the half-finished bottle. "What the heck?" She narrowed her eyes and whispered urgently. "How long has he been asleep, Alexander?"

"I don't know, a few minutes?" He didn't seem too sure. But he continued studying her face. "Will he be alright, or should we burp him?"

"No, I don't know. I'll call Gemma, or better still, you call her and she won't know that I'm here."

He frowned and his bespectacled green eyes darkened. "Why? You don't want to be seen with me?"

At her steady stare, he shrugged, "Okay, I don't blame you." He sighed, "And I *am* sorry...." His expression alert he asked, "Did I interrupt your date tonight?" The serious glare turned dangerous and she saw a glimpse of the iron will he must have forged and learned to use in business.

"Maybe. But it's none of your business." Then feeling like a fraud she said, "No, but should we call Gemma?"

"No." The playful enigmatic Alexander resurfaced. "I'll see if this works." He put the bottle against the baby's pouty lips and Jordan started to suck. His eyes fluttered open slightly as his uncle said softly, "Ah, we're in business."

Relieved, she wondered—or wished perhaps—if this was part

of another ploy for him to spend time with her. *No, don't be so suspicious, or a hopeful romantic,* she reprimanded herself.

When Jordan finished the rest of the bottle, Alexander tried to pick him up gently, gingerly as if handling a delicate live doll.

Well, he was, Olivia reminded herself in awe!

She still couldn't believe how brave and natural Maria and Sloan and Gemma and Grey were with their children. Maria had simply said one word when asked about how she and Sloan managed it without completely losing their sanity, worrying about every aspect of keeping kids safe and happy.

"Love." To which Gemma had added, "And faith that everything will work out and be all right."

Olivia reminded herself to breathe and stay calm. And not tread down that wistful road of '*what if's*.

Within a couple of minutes of leaning over his uncle's broad shoulder, which was covered by a small towel, Jordan gave a gentle belch. Only then did Alexander's large hand stop the obviously calming patting on the baby's little back and shoulders.

Something deep within Olivia shifted and she got up to ostensibly get herself a glass of water. She could hardly swallow through the lump of emotion wedged in her throat.

Alexander looked so lovely and comfortable with a baby in his arms that this time she couldn't stop herself from imagining a lucky, gorgeous Greek wife giving him dark haired, beautiful babies.

It was almost her undoing.

CHAPTER 11

Olivia got her bag and started towards the front door. She had to leave, now. "Well, take care and bye."

"Why are you in such a rush?" Alexander whispered while holding Jordan. "Am I such a bore or…a danger to you?"

Without turning she said, "Neither, and I have to finish some things."

"I'd like to take you to dinner tomorrow night as a thank you."

"No, thanks. And no need, I came for Jordan's sake, and it was a . . . learning experience."

"I insist, Olivia." He was behind her. When she peeked over her shoulder Jordan was in his crib and Alexander watched her with those knowing eyes.

"No, thanks." She said firmly. Whether there was another girl or not, he was still as immature as she remembered, and she didn't need any complications with any man, least of all him.

He touched her arms, stopping her from turning away from him and observed her, "But I insist, and I won't take no for an answer."

"You'll just have to, this time. Sorry."

"I'm trying to make amends, Olivia. I really am."

"Only if you tell me the truth."

He raised an eyebrow and she asked, "Did you do this to get me here? Do you really know how to take care of a baby?"

The silence grew as they stared at each other. "If I said yes I did and I do, will you storm out of here and away from me like you always do?"

"I'm not the one who ran away to Greece the night before an important gala. Not even a goodbye, after we'd shared so much, and you'd even said that you l…" She stared at him, annoyed to have her suspicions confirmed. Taking in a steadying breath she added, "But many guys will say anything to get what they want. And I hope this isn't the way you conduct business."

He glanced down for a moment and then studied her face, "That's not true. I've never said 'I love you' to any other woman I was with."

How could she feel like a hot, squishy marshmallow inside just hearing those words?

Put yourself together, girl!

"I was a coward and an idiot back then and a few days ago. I know you deserve better and the truth." He said slowly. "I apologize again and I want to make up for it now, Olivia."

"I'm not interested in anything other than my work at this time of my life."

"But fate has brought us together, Olivia. I know you still feel the connection between us. And don't even say that it's nothing but a first crush. We both know it's way more than that. Always has been."

She shook her head, feeling that twisting hunger deep inside her. But just as quickly it was replaced by something else. She couldn't risk being hurt again. She couldn't handle rejection again by the one man who…

"I'll think about it." But she saw from his expression that he didn't buy it.

But this was not cowardice on her part. It was self-preservation.

"You won't make it easy for me, will you?"

"Can you blame me, Alexander?"

He sighed and shrugged, "Fair enough. Tell me what I have to do."

"See this as a business deal where the other party needs more proof of your integrity." She shrugged and waved. "Bye."

~

A happy bubble surrounded Alex, leaving him feeling elated. Olivia was here, dining with him and having a relaxed time without that thunderous expression of wanting to strangle him. He had finally risked the truth and despite his last week's babysitting ruse, the generous, forgiving woman had given him a second chance. Or was this a third chance?

Don't blow it this time.

He would take every opportunity to see her at the beach house as well as spend any spare time she would give him. His business would manage without him for another short while, and for the first time since he could remember the idea of returning to Greece and to his business held little appeal.

Alex delayed his return flight for another two weeks.

Fortunately for him, his corporation was a well-oiled machine with trusted, committed employees. Although his father was officially semi retired, the fifty-nine-year-old Costa Kyriakou still was as active as he had always been especially while Alex was away.

When he told his father of his delay in returning he was greeted with silence at the other end of the line.

"This is unlike you, Alexos. You sure you're all right?"

"Of course, never better. I'm just taking time to enjoy... I'm still on top of everything through email, and between you and Adrian—I won't be missed."

"I was supposed to be fully retired by now, Alexos. Even staying at your Athens place it's tiring to keep up with the pace."

Alex chuckled, "We both know that you love it. You just like to make a fuss and complain about doing all the work, when we both know that you'd be bored out of your mind at the villa without all the hustle and bustle."

Alex knew that his father loved being part of the busy enterprise and always would. He saw how much he enjoyed Grey's business visits every few months, when they discussed everything from politics to global economy and how 'you, the boys' could continue making a difference in the world.

His father had always dreamed Alex would one day take over the business. Alex had done that and grown it to newer heights. He wanted to make him proud.

"Besides, I'm taking care of something important here, right now. So I appreciate your help in keeping everything on an even keel."

"Sounds intriguing, son. Care to share?"

"Not yet, but suffice it to say, you'll be happy to hear that your son is taking the right kind of risks outside of the business arena."

The chuckle so much like his own reverberated over the line. "So you're listening to your father and going after love! So I can look forward to becoming a grandfather in my sixties after all?"

"One step at a time, Papa, but I'm going in the right direction."

"Good, you're finally growing up."

Now, here in Wrightsville Beach, so close to Olivia, business was the last thing on his mind. He studied her flushed face as she shared with him her remaining ideas about Aunt Jenny's beach house renovation and wanted to lose himself in her eyes, in her arms….

Patience, he reminded himself, *Olivia is worth it.*

CHAPTER 12

Over the past few days since Olivia had given Alexander another chance, he had spent most of his time with her, including during her working hours at the beach house.

"That's a nice touch, Alexander. I didn't know you have such a good eye. I should have known. We'll go with that, definitely." She smiled at his suggestion to expand the small custom bookcase further towards the TV.

Olivia found herself sharing her ideas about the decor and the style she and Maria had envisioned for the place.

With every day they bonded over many different things, while instead of distracting her, Alexander continued to be a great asset to the nearly completed redesign project. Yesterday he had suggested placing the perfectly reupholstered, cream jacquard antique wing chair by the large window. As soon as he had said it, Olivia felt goose bumps. It was a great idea.

Aunt Jenny would have loved her favorite armchair to be used in the new reading nook, watching the world and clouds go by over the changing tides.

Echoing Maria, Alexander also encouraged Olivia to go with

her own gut and personal choices, even though the Ellis cottage was being prepared for sale.

When the kitchen appliances were delivered, Alexander pulled up his sleeves and heaved the huge, hefty oven along with the other four workers, proving to her just how physically strong he was. And how ready he was to help in any way he could.

She tried not to stare but the hero worship which had taken hold of her after his award acceptance speech now grew despite her determination not to be affected by him.

In the style of an ever-retreating superhero after saving the day, Alexander didn't want any gratitude or reward. As if helping and saving the day were no big deal and all part of who he was.

She was even more impressed with his cool calm this morning, when Alexander had managed to salvage an otherwise difficult situation with one of the electricians who had not turned up yesterday, and had now caused some delays with the kitchen appliance installation.

Without being aware of it, Alexander made a mockery of Olivia's earlier accusation of him being a male chauvinist.

"Ms. Moore, I can't help that I was unavailable last week, so I'm here now, what's the big deal?" The rugged, short man with a protruding belly and over loaded denim pockets, whistled through his crooked mouth.

When Olivia didn't answer he said, "You designers don't know everything. Sure you want it to look a certain way, but the technical aspects of what goes on behind the walls; you should leave to us, the experts. So I say it again, just so we're clear. I'll do the rewiring, I'll do it the way I know it should be done, and not the way you think it has to be done. And it'll cost an extra $2,500. Payable before I start."

"And let me explain about how I feel about extortion, Mr. Springhead." Olivia was about to blow a fuse inside her thumping head when she felt Alexander's hand on her upper arm.

She glanced at him, forcing herself to relax, somehow feeling empowered just by his presence.

"I'm Alexander Anderson, Ms. Moore's business and legal advisor. I heard the unfortunate situation and I'd like to have a word with you Mr. Springhead, if I may."

The wide-girthed electrician paled somewhat but brought himself up a whole inch taller than his five-feet-seven, hooked his thumbs on his crooked tool belt and inclined his head to his right. "As I say…"

"Yes, I think both Ms. Moore and I quite understand what you 'say'." Alexander said smoothly. The steel firmness didn't go unnoticed on Olivia.

He must be an amazing powerhouse in business, was all she thought as she watched the interaction between the bald electrician and the tall handsome Alexander.

She almost missed their conversation so intent on the electrician's change of body language as Alexander continued to speak softly yet clearly.

"So as I say, Ms. Moore is your boss, and your contract stipulates that you cover all the unforeseen expenses through this project. Is that correct?"

"Well, but this is different."

"We all know that you have two choices right now. You either finish the work, and I'll have my own guy oversee everything as you do it, or you walk away right now."

Mr. Springhead spluttered, literally reddening from his head into the first unbuttoned shirt, "I don't like to leave a job half finished, but I've not been paid $4,700 for this part of—"

"That's right. So it's up to you. We live in a country of free speech and free choice." Then looking to his left, he added, "Ah, here is Peter, my own electrician who's willing and able to take over your work. Or you agree to finish what you were contracted to do by end of today. Just the way Ms. Moore had stipulated."

Mr. Springhead looked like a wounded cowering criminal by

the time Alexander had added, "Good choice. I knew we'd come to a mutually agreeable compromise. And I'll be following your career from now on and if I see any reviews or complaints about your underhanded business dealings, rest assured I'll be coming after you. And I won't be as magnanimous as I'm being at present." He leaned in to the man's face and asked, "Is that understood, Mr. Springhead?"

All the electrician did was nod with his red face making it quite clear what he thought of the interfering 'legal advisor'.

Olivia closed her mouth as she watched Alexander.

She was seeing yet another fascinating aspect of him, confirming that her instincts about him were right. He was the whole package, and a very unique man who knew how to be gentle with a baby—and he'd known what he was doing all along, damn him—while being firm and unrelenting in business.

His sense of justice mirrored her own.

~

*L*etting the afternoon sun dry their ocean soaked skin on beach towels Alexander turned his face to her and said softly, "It's so effortless talking to you, always has been. Just being together—"

"Don't…" She didn't want to revisit anything that personal. She was going with the flow and having fun. "Let's just enjoy the time together. It made her feel on edge whenever he posed questions she did not want to contemplate about life and her future which she hadn't accounted for.

Even spending this time together left her confused and terrified about where it could lead. There was no place for romance or any of its complications in her adult life.

Her suddenly resurfaced sexual libido was making it increasingly difficult. Although she enjoyed his company she found herself too uncomfortably aware of his manly build whenever they went swimming together. Invariably her dreams would replay how masculine he was, and how he filled out those swim trunks. Inevitably a scene from their first time in the linen closet would grow into a dramatic love scene in a gorgeous regal bed...

Right now, his discreet glances at her form also made her too aware of how attractive he found her, too.

"So why didn't you attend Maria and Sloan's wedding? It wasn't because of me, was it?"

She shook her head, "No, of course not. Do you think that would have stopped me from coming to my BFF's most special day? I'd have given anything to be there."

"No, I suppose that sounded stupid." Alexander said. "Then what was it? Maria said you were recovering from some temporary illness."

"That's exactly what it was." Afraid what she would unintentionally divulge to him, she determined to change the subject and steered it back to discuss the finishing touches of the renovation.

She was truly gratified that Alexander respected her reticence and let it go.

CHAPTER 13

"You have to admit that you and Alexander have amazing chemistry together." Maria smiled at Olivia as they gathered up and rolled their yoga mats after another reinvigorating and yet relaxing session.

Olivia replaced her mat inside its carrier and with both her hands free she readjusted her red hair in a fresh ponytail. "You can't say anything to anyone—"

"Hey, what can't she say to anyone?" Gemma appeared from behind Olivia. "Is it that you're spending more time with our Alexander?" Gemma's eyes held that same sparkle.

"We're just…just friends."

Maria chuckled, "Don't kid us married women. We can see through all the armor. And why are you so afraid anyway? You've always had a thing for him, and he's here now and he's even delayed his return to Greece."

"What do you mean 'always had a thing', Maria?" Gemma's curiosity was obviously spiked and Olivia sighed as she briskly started walking away from them.

"Let Liv tell you about it." Maria said as they followed her.

"I smell a romantic story, Olivia." Gemma caught up and

84

weaved her free arm through Olivia's elbow. "Let's have a coffee before we get back to our mundane lives."

"Right, you and Maria have the most boring and mundane lives in the world filled with adoring husbands and adorable babies." Olivia smiled and rolled her eyes.

"Well, if you play your cards right you may become our official sister." Gemma almost squealed and added, "Wouldn't that be fab, Maria?"

"Absolutely what I'm counting on." Maria nodded with her own bright smile.

"So stop wasting time and give," Gemma demanded, "You know me well enough by now to realize it's futile to argue. I'll just make a quick call to Grey, he owes me."

Despite her hesitation and even fear to think about anything that was unfolding and developing between Alexander and herself, Olivia admitted to herself how much she needed to talk about her feelings and the newness of it all with her best friend and her newest pal who seemed to understand Olivia so well.

Half an hour later they sat laughing in the quieter corner of the café as Olivia told Gemma the shortened version of her summer romance with Alexander a decade ago. Maria peppered the story with her own romanticized additions until Olivia squirmed and blushed.

As Olivia finished explaining about the convoluted plan Alexander had concocted and how it had blown up in his face, Maria shook her head, "He was too afraid to do this the adult way. I'm shocked. He's so forthright in business and I've seen him in action…But obviously you forgave him otherwise he wouldn't be spending so much time around the cottage and wooing you. This is so dreamy."

"You're such a romantic, Maria, stop it." Olivia said but liked hearing the words. "We're just spending time together, that's all."

"I knew he was up to something when he offered to babysit Tyler that night." Gemma shook her head, grinning. "I've always liked the Anderson brothers' determination to succeed in anything they put their minds on."

"And our last single brother-in-law has got his sights on *you*." Maria's grin bloomed.

"No he doesn't." Olivia felt her cheeks grow red.

"Yes he does. So how do *you* feel about him? He's so caring and quite handsome. And so sexy in his geeky way." Maria raised her brow in that comical way.

Finally Olivia gave in and smiled, "I find his brain as sexy and a turn-on as much as the rest of him."

"Now we're getting somewhere." Gemma laughed. "So how far have you gone?"

"I'm not going to answer that." Olivia clammed her lips together as she grew warmer in her face and down towards her breasts.

"They jog together every morning," Maria explained to Gemma. "They go swimming and he takes her out but she insists on paying her half."

"We have a lot to talk about, catching up and sharing about our lives."

Gemma smirked, "And what else do you do?"

"We're just—"

"Friends. Yes I know." Maria said. Leaning closer, her eyes filled with concern, "Have you told him about the…"

"That I conquered breast cancer? No, it's not appropriate really, and it's all behind me anyway."

"It's not as if he won't understand." Gemma said. "He's one of the most caring men I've ever met, like all the Anderson brothers. It's in their DNA and nurturing." Gemma put her hand on Olivia's on top of the small table. "So has he invited you to the barbecue party on Saturday yet?"

Olivia shook her head, "I wouldn't feel comfortable coming to it even if he did."

"But he's leaving in a week and a bit, isn't he?"

She nodded, "That's why I'm trying to focus on my work and not have any expectations."

"But doesn't *he* have any? I can see it in his eyes. He's got it bad for you," Maria said. "And he's a one woman kind of man like his brothers. And Sloan said that he's never seen Alexander this happy."

"And Grey said that Alexander had asked him for advice about buying more investment properties here."

Despite her treacherous naïve heart, which leapt and skipped inside her chest, she said, "That has nothing to do with me, it's also in the Anderson Brothers' business DNA."

"Yes, that's what you'd think." Maria said. "You're just being chicken."

"Look, I have no answers for you. I'm trying to go with the flow and not plan ahead too much in this arena. I'd not even wanted to think about anything…"

"You can't even say it; it's romance, and it's okay to contemplate having a warm and loving relationship with a likeminded man." Maria said.

"Tell us if you need any advice or anything." Gemma prompted. "This is so exciting. Can you imagine it, Maria? We could be having another Anderson wedding within the next year."

"That would be perf—"

"Whoa!" Olivia almost stood up. "Get a hold of your imaginations, ladies! I'm getting very scared indeed right now."

Both her friends clucked like hens at the same time and burst out giggling like teenagers. Olivia couldn't help but feel the mirth within her, too.

Her smile grew into hearty laughter despite her fear.

All she knew was that when she spent time with Alexander he stimulated her mind, entertained her with his wit and sense of humor, asked her probing questions which made her wonder about the future, and she felt hope blossom.

They were so in tune with each other.

Sometimes he simply hugged her as if aware she was open to it, but never pushed himself on her in a sexual way. She appreciated him, and loved those days when instead of making her laugh with yet another story about his family or a business anecdote, Alexander would run in companionable silence beside her.

"All I'll say is that Alexander is a very special human being." Maria said and Gemma nodded.

Olivia knew that, but there were still too many unsaid things between her and Alexander.

CHAPTER 14

O livia stared at the beautiful seascape through the window of one of the smaller bedrooms in Aunt Jenny's nearly completed cottage. Alexander stood beside her. Glancing sideways and up at him she said, "The owners can instantly turn this study/guest room into a nursery by painting the room with a soft, sunny yellow and replacing the furniture with a sweet crib and..."

Alexander's expression stopped her words. He looked like he did back at twenty, the romantic gleam in his eyes shining with hope. He may as well have worn a neon sign across his chest saying; *Wouldn't it be amazing if you and I were the owners, and bringing up babies here together?*

As he closed the gap between them she prayed she wouldn't swoon if he touched her. Because she had been obsessing about him and his kisses for too long.

His mouth stopped a breath away from hers but he didn't come any closer, as if waiting for her consent. Yet wasn't he aware she yearned for his thorough kiss? His eyes sparkled with a touch of humor as he asked softly, "How many children do you think...?"

Unable to trust herself to speak, she concentrated on taking in a small breath and releasing it. "The family can fit four children, with bunk beds in two of the rooms."

"Or they could have one girl and one boy and then spend more time traveling together. Perhaps to their villa in some hidden part of Greece..." He studied her eyes and she tried to look away but couldn't.

"Don't look at me like that." Her voice sounded strained.

Could he see right through her? Her hope, her fear, her hunger for him?

He wouldn't break eye contact and she was beginning to feel light headed. Not trusting her voice or her body to betray her she started turning away from him. But he wouldn't have it.

Holding her chin tenderly between thumb and the crook of his index finger Alexander stared down at her lips. She felt their magnetic pull towards each other's mouths.

But he still didn't kiss her.

She wanted to scream with need but felt compelled to scan his face as he asked, "They can have a Corgi for her and one large Golden lab for him."

He remembered her favorite choice of ideal pet. The sweet, romantic fool. As she was about to throw her arms around him he added, "Sound good to you?" This time he sounded slightly gruff, which gladdened her that she wasn't the only one suffering, wanting, needing.

What was the question among all that dreaming? She replayed it in her mind and whispered, "Yes, it does sound perfect...this as a permanent home, with another place in Greece."

"I love it here." Then he slowly closed the space between their lips and she moved in and raised her lips to his. And finally they were kissing again.

She sighed and melted into him as if it was where she belonged, and intertwined her arms around his neck, enjoying his familiar fresh and manly scent.

He held her tighter as she deepened their kiss.

Many minutes passed, she couldn't be sure how long, but the soft knock on the open door forced Alexander to slowly pull his mouth away from hers. Just as reluctantly his arms loosened around her, letting her step away from him.

It hadn't been nearly enough for her, darn it. The regret and disappointment in his green eyes confirmed he agreed with her, promising of what was yet to come.

"I'll see you later at seven, Olivia. Or we can meet earlier and have a quick swim." He said in a low voice before letting her go completely.

"That sounds good." She smiled.

"See you at six then."

Then he left her to try and concentrate on the worker's urgent question.

～

*N*ow, with only a couple of days left before his return to Athens, Olivia was not going to miss her opportunity to be with Alexander; to feel that special bond in all possible ways. The sense of inevitability grew as he walked her to her hotel room door after yet another delicious and fun dinner date together. Only this time she wanted him to stay. She needed Alexander to kiss her, hold her, and to finish what they had started earlier.

She'd looked forward to his kisses so much she ached inside, and opening her door she turned and smiled up at him and felt that betraying heat burn her face and neck. "You want to come in?"

He grinned as if she had asked a silly question. Before they had even closed the door behind them they were hugging, their mouths and tongues exploring while laughing softly. Relief emanated from him. They shuffled their way in the soft lamplight towards the waiting bed.

At its edge she stood looking up at Alexander as he slowly weaved one large hand around her arm and cupped her cheek.

CHAPTER 15

Almost all their clothes were strewn on the floor around them, and as their eyes met again Alexander's expression singed her from the inside out. He stroked her skin reverently, as if he couldn't get enough of seeing and touching her. Her breasts felt heavy against her black bra.

"I can't believe how soft and delicious you are. You're so beautiful, Olivia." He said roughly, as she marveled at his large, bare torso, his masculine physique which he seemed to take for granted. How could he have hidden all this glory away for so long until she had insisted he change his style? Since their swim sessions over the past couple of weeks her dreams had been vividly fueled by his magnificence.

Her trembling fingers stroked the dark chest hairs. As his deft fingers touched the bra clasp between her breasts she stopped him.

"No lights," she said unevenly and retreated towards the lamp on the nightstand.

"But I want to see you, to watch those eyes as we..." He followed her as if he couldn't bear being apart from her anymore.

Her fear must have shown just before she switched off the

light, because he whispered, "But it's okay, maybe later." As darkness enveloped them he drew open the curtains to let some natural night lights filter through the sheers. She heard him placing his glasses off and putting them neatly on the nightstand as he added, "As long as you don't kick me out till tomorrow, Olivia. I've been dreaming of being with you for far too long." His mouth was poised over hers, and she answered with her lips grinding against his. Opening herself up to him completely.

Then their hunger took over and she let herself feel and not question anything. She definitely refused to think about time and distance between them after his imminent departure in a few days.

The here and now was all that anyone ever had.

~

"You feel so good against me, so perfect. I've wanted to do this for so long, *agápi mou*." Alex pulled her naked curves into him knowing full well that this was the first time he had ever said the Greek endearment which meant 'my darling' or 'my love,' and he meant it.

Then they were lost in each other. In the darkness his other senses sharpened. Attuned to her soft moans he explored with his fingers and tongue the many wonders of Olivia's body and the divine curves he'd hungered for; especially after seeing her in her one piece black swimsuit. The demure outfit had accentuated her curves to perfection.

Now in his mind's eye he could see just how lush and heavy her breasts were, as he tasted them reverently. Laying beside her he heard her heart pounding as loudly as he felt his own drum within his chest. As he molded her buttocks in his hands to bring her even closer into himself he couldn't get enough of her sensuous scent. The fragrance of crushed flowers mingled with the seductive lavender which always transported him back to that linen closet.

His groan echoed within his chest, feeling as if this was their very first time and yet like they have never been apart.

For the past decade he had craved to be this in sync with Olivia. He had thought he had lost her forever. Now no one else would ever do. Through his heated thoughts and swelling pleasure, he knew without a doubt that this was much more than merely a physical joining.

Wanting her so desperately he sheathed himself right now. Despite his escalating desire for her he would make it wonderful for Olivia. He lifted her gently on top of himself and found her moist and hot center. She was so hot and ready for him that he prayed for patience, reminding himself that he had self control.

But it was touch and go as she seemed to implode, and as her breathing became erratic she grabbed his upper arms as she called out his name. Then the orgasm overtook her completely and her breasts and warm abdomen crushed against him. He kissed her, soaking in her moans.

Bringing Olivia to orgasm he wished he could see her, loving every single moment of how completely she let herself go, how much she trusted him, after all.

Gently rolling her onto her back he braced himself above her. He kissed her and explored her mouth as he entered her slowly. As she breathed in and opened herself even more to him he plunged deeper into her. She tightened her legs around his waist and the satisfied and growing moans surrounded them. Then the urge within her rose and tightened around him again, and all he wanted was to stay in this nirvana forever.

～

*S*weat cooling on both their sated bodies as Alex lay breathless next to the incredibly sensuous Olivia, all he could think was, *this is magic!*

He had known a few women, but all these years what had been missing was this all-important piece of the jigsaw puzzle. His heart had not been as involved as it was here, right now. This was not merely great sex, it was everything making love ought to be. This was the component which had defeated even his youngest brother, the once die-hard bachelor, Grey, as well as his other brothers.

Love was too powerful to resist or even fight.

CHAPTER 16

*O*livia had finally agreed to come to the Andersons' family pool party. Alexander had promised that she could leave at any time if she felt at all uncomfortable.

As they entered through the wide side open gates she took in a steadying breath and reminded herself that she would have attended the party as Maria and Gemma's friend. No one needed to know that she was spending time with Alexander in any romantic way.

Therefore she repeated what she had said in the car on the way over, "Please just go and mingle and don't be stuck to my side. I'm a big girl and can look after myself. I'll just be part of the party."

"Without bringing any extra attention to yourself." He said softly in her ear. When she pushed him away from herself afraid they would be seen, he merely smiled. "One would think you're embarrassed to be seen with me. I'll have you know I'm one of *the* Anderson brothers. Our reputation is world renowned—"

"Please go or I'll—"

"OK, you obstinate woman whom I can't wait to bed again and make you melt in my arms…"

"Are you seriously doing this right now?" Olivia trembled inside at the evocative visual he was painting in her mind. She glanced away from him, and scoured the faces interspersed across the dark green meadows of the large Anderson estate.

"So you don't want me to introduce you to anyone as my…"

"I'm regretting agreeing to come with you." At his deliberate lascivious look into her eyes she nearly turned round to go back to her car.

"OK." He discreetly grabbed her hand by the skirt of her flowy summer dress and stopped her. "Sorry, I promise to be a good boy and not have any more fun at your expense."

He tried to erase the amusement from his face but she saw that it was proving too difficult.

Then he made slow work of moving away from her as he said, "I'll give you fifteen minutes and then I'll bring you a cold glass of wine. Unless you want something stronger?"

His lopsided grin made her smile and say, "Not a good idea, but thanks for the thought. Wine will be lovely, thanks."

With one last look at her he strolled away towards a laughing group of young people to their right.

Although more people were coming through the side of the house, the feast was in full swing and she recognized some other Anderson brothers she had already met, as they chatted and drank beer and other refreshments under the hot sun or in the shade of the great umbrellas closely interspersed across the large open space. Many people were enjoying the incredible spread Sandra and her daughters-in-law had organized. Her culinary reputation was well known in Wrightsville Beach.

Olivia resolved to relax and enjoy every minute of the jovial atmosphere.

Accepting a tall ice-filled fruity looking glass she made her way in the opposite direction from Alexander and some of his other brothers and wives.

As she turned to watch and listen to the shrieking kids splashing a few feet away in the shallow end of the large azure-blue pool, she caught Alexander's glance and tried to look around as non-challantly as she could.

Despite the hustle of her beautiful surroundings her eyes seemed to land on Alexander, knowing automatically where he was. He seemed to always position himself to be facing her way, near and yet far away enough for her comfort. He would glance at her while paying attention to whoever he was speaking with at the time.

A few feet further back from Alexander's clutch of people she saw Maria next to Sloan, naturally holding each other by their waists.

Olivia soaked in the happy ambiance, imagining what would have happened if she had never met Alexander in her teens and then met him now for the first time at this party. Would she have been as hesitant about trusting him? Would she have given herself to him as completely as she had in her teens in the name of love?

She would never know. On the other hand knowing Alexander in her teens gave her an advantage. She had a better idea of who he had now become.

All she had was the present, she reminded herself, on this beautiful sunny day with perfect picnic weather and hearty children's laughter and family and friends who all seemed to know each other well.

"Hey you," Maria came to Olivia with an older blonde woman, whose attractive blue eyes seemed to have the same color and astuteness as Sloan's. "Olivia, meet my mother-in-law, Sandra."

Olivia felt the observant eyes scan her face as they shook hands. "It's so *very* nice to meet you at last, Olivia."

Had Alexander said anything about her? She couldn't imagine it. A quick glance in his direction confirmed that he was still watching her with that curious expression. Now he was joined by Wyatt and Logan whom she recognized from Maria's wedding photographs and in the various gossip magazines.

The Anderson brothers were as good looking as the cast of an all star Hollywood movie, Olivia thought with a smile, trying to tear her gaze away from Alexander's vicinity.

"Maria has told me so much about her best friend in the whole wide world." Sandra smiled and the radiant joy in her face eliminated any reservations Olivia may have had about coming.

As Gemma neared them and hugged her, Olivia sent out a little prayer that they would keep their last week's girly chat to themselves.

"I thought *I'm* your best friend in the whole wide world," Gemma said to Maria with a light curve of her eyebrows. "But as you're such a good sister-in-law I'll share you with Olivia. She's not so bad." She hugged Olivia again and whispered, "I'm so glad you didn't chicken out."

Olivia smiled at her and nodded. "It's lovely, I'm glad I came. It's a wonderful spread, Mrs. Anderson. And I've heard what a lovely mother-in-law you are."

"That's sweet," Sandra reached out both her hands to her daughters-in-law and cupped their faces in the most natural way as if they were her own daughters. "They make my boys very happy and they're pretty and smart to boot. And as long as they give me grandkids I'm not complaining."

Olivia saw where Alexander got his sense of humor and wit from.

"You have to meet my husband, Jason. He was here a moment ago...Oh, there he is, supervising the barbecue. Should have known. Let's go girls and save some burgers."

The older woman's playful grin encapsulated all the affection and pride in a long-loved spouse. The warmth made Olivia so happy for Maria and Gemma. A deep secret part of her wished it was something she could one day experience. This kind of bond, ease and respect for each other.

Here romance lived in peace and harmony with great dollops of joy and laughter brought through grandchildren and growing extended families.

"Actually, Olivia, first I'd like you to meet the rest of the boys."

Oh no, what if Sandra introduced Alexander to her? How would…

"So she's met Sloan and Grey," Gemma said.

"Hey, Olivia," they both smiled at her as their mother then looked up at Alexander

"And here's my youngest, Alexander, whom—"

"Hello," Alexander said without missing a beat, and leaning into Olivia's personal space. The twinkle in his eyes made her want to stomp on his foot or at least say something that would wipe off that smirk.

Nothing came to mind as Sandra's astute gaze switched from Olivia to Alexander. The older woman probably saw much more than Olivia wanted her to.

"What a lovely name. Olivia. So you're Maria's best friend. Never knew she had such a lovely friend, otherwise I'd have asked her to hook us up."

At this Sandra raised an eyebrow. "You don't have to pretend on my behalf, Alex. I saw you two come in, and I might add, you looked adorable together. And if I hadn't seen you arrive I'd have been tipped off by your language. You'd never ask anyone to 'hook you up' with anyone." Sandra almost laughed at her son's grin and blush at the cheeks above his lean beard and his deeply tanned throat. "So after I introduce Olivia to your father you two can just go ahead and enjoy yourselves, with no pretences necessary."

The adorable tall man looked sheepish and proud at the same time as he watched her being towed away.

"I should have known nothing passes by you, Mom." His hug enveloped the short woman as he leaned down to hold her.

"You know mothers have eyes at the back of their heads." Maria said and her smile beamed even more brightly than Gemma's, whose effervescent energy emanated from her hooked elbow through Olivia's whole body.

She allowed herself to be maneuvered towards a tall older version of what she imagined Sloan or Grey would look like in twenty or so years.

The slim, handsome man with broad shoulders and a head of silver blond hair glanced up with his metal spatula above the barbecue grill. As they approached the man's eyes creased at the corners as his face took on that same soft expression Olivia remembered on her father's face whenever he saw her mother come into the room.

"Jason, I have someone very special for you to meet. Olivia is Maria's best friend."

"Ah, the designer who's doing a fabulous job at her grandmother's little cottage, I hear." His smile broadened as he added, "Another beautiful young woman. This party gets better and better. What with the news...Do you know about Logan and Katie's—" He asked his daughters-in-law and wife.

"Shh, Jason," Sandra lowered her voice in the hubbub quickly scanning the nearby crowd. "They want to announce it themselves later."

"Okay, got it." Jason clamped his lips dramatically. But a wide grin escaped as he leaned into his wife. Olivia found it adorable the way they naturally gravitated towards each other and Sandra accepted his peck on the cheek.

Gemma and Maria gave Olivia that special glance which made her face grow hot and she felt rather than saw Alexander nearby.

"Jason, I hear Martin is already too unsteady on his feet. So please go and take care of your high-maintenance brother."

Sandra nodded and reached for his prized spatula. "Don't worry, I'll take over your barbecue responsibilities. You just go and enjoy."

As Jason strode away looking for his brother Sandra leaned closer to Olivia and said, "He thinks he's the best griller in Wrightsville Beach, and I let him think so, but in reality he over cooks everything. And we only want juicy burgers, right?"

"Ah, okay, be right there." Gemma closed her cell phone. "That's Lee, I'll just go and help the babysitter find Jordan's swim stuff and bring him out."

"Let me do that." Alexander popped his head to her peripheral vision. "I know, I know, he's just woken up from his nap and he'll be grumpy. I've got this."

"Oooh," Maria smiled, "Trying to impress Olivia. Is it working?"

Olivia rolled her eyes and said, "It only reminds me of the stunt he pulled by pretending not to know how to babysit Jordan that night. To get me to 'help him out of a jam.'"

Sandra burst out laughing, "Still up to your old tricks, Alex?"

Alexander turned back and stopped a few feet away from the women. "I don't know what you're talking about." And with a warning glance at his mother said, "Please don't embarrass me, Mom. Promise?"

That vulnerable look in his green eyes made Olivia fall in love with him just a little bit more.

"Can't do that, Alex, all part of my role. Now go and bring back my grandson number two."

As the women chatted time seemed to disappear. Mother-in-law and her two daughters-in-law caught each other up as if they had known each other always. Olivia couldn't imagine that kind of bond. They laughed discreetly, including her in their light and harmless gossip. They giggled about a single cousin's blind date disaster which involved a man's toupee being dislodged by a waiter's tray, and about who would end up making a bigger fool of themselves by the end of the evening; Aunty Grace, who was not in the least graceful, or Uncle Martin who was already becoming teary and emotional with his, "I love you, man, and I love you sooo mush."

Olivia was also honored that they trusted her with the news that Logan and Katie, the second Anderson brother and his lovely wife planned to announce their news later today; they were expecting twins in the spring of next year. "They hadn't wanted to say anything until after the thirteenth week had passed." Maria smiled.

"Oh, I don't blame them one bit." Gemma shook her head. "I remember how nerve racking those first few weeks can be. Exciting but nevertheless…"

"Especially Katie told me last night that they'd tried for quite a while before they finally got pregnant. They'll be fantastic parents." Maria said. "I'm so excited for them. More cousins for Tyler and Jordan to play with."

"And for Sandra to make more fuss over." Gemma nodded.

"I'm over the moon. So," Sandra said, "That only leaves Wyatt and Laine to make me a proud grandmother in the next year or two once they've finally settled down from all that exotic traveling. Unless," Sandra peered at Olivia with a smile, "Alex surprises us all and beats them with his own news."

Olivia tried to distract her mind with something else, anything that would stop the heat in her face and neck from betraying her embarrassment. How could she not take this personally?

"There's Jordan. Ah, looks like Alex wants our boy to say hello to his daddy." Gemma smiled with that sparkle in her eyes. "Okay, Maria and I will introduce Olivia to the rest of the gang. I see Wyatt and Laine are with our guys now." Gemma kissed Sandra's cheek and was already pulling them gently along towards the Anderson brothers who seemed to naturally reconnect like best friends.

As Olivia watched yet another good looking brother sharing a bottle of beer and his gorgeous wife, Laine hold a wine glass, she heard Gemma say over her shoulder, "Give us the sign when the meat's ready for serving, Sandra and we'll give you a hand."

As Olivia walked between Gemma and Maria towards the group where her lover stood—she felt her whole body grow weak, *OMG, Alexander is my lover*—she admired the way he held baby Jordan so effortlessly in his arms.

As they neared the men Gemma took a quick photograph with her cell phone and said, "Oh, isn't that a perfect memory in the making? I'll text you and Sandra the photos later, Maria."

She focused on Alexander whose full attention was on his nephew just as the baby's fists grabbed his dark beard and his golden head seemed to gravitate towards Alexander's nose.

Olivia watched as Jordan's open mouth landed on Alex's nose and sucked on it.

Smiling, taking it in his stride she heard Alexander say, "Yes, I love you too, bud. And look, here's your daddy." Laughing he disengaged his nephew's tiny clutching fingers and gently relegated the bundle into his oldest brother's arms. "I changed his diaper and paid the babysitter, so next dinner's on you, bro."

"He's fascinated by your Neanderthal beard." Sloan grinned as Jordan threw his arms around his neck and settled on top of his large shoulders.

"It's called style, bro, some of us are still single and trying to impress—" His words stopped as he turned and obviously saw the oncoming entourage.

Only three feet away from them now, for a split second Olivia visualized what it would feel like to be making her way to him in a flowing, white princess dress down the grassy path towards a custom rose and lily covered arbor, with her best friends as her maids of honor slowly bringing her towards her lover who would soon become her…

Get a grip, Olivia. Focus on the present. There were many obstacles like geographical and logistic ones if it ever came to that.

She gritted her teeth and tried to smile but something in Alexander's widening eyes and betraying grin, made her break eye contact with him. She prayed he couldn't read her thoughts on her face.

CHAPTER 17

It had been the most delicious, glorious week of his life. It felt perfect being with Olivia.

As a bonus Alex's family liked her just like he knew they would. Mom had told him after the party, "Make me proud and follow your heart. We can all see how you fit so well together. Follow your brothers' lead and we may have another wedding soon."

The tingles inside him shook him up a bit, "First things first, Mom. I plan to invite Olivia to spend more time with me in Athens and introduce her to Papa."

"You know he'll love her."

Alex knew that Papa would be ecstatic just to discover that Alex was dating, never mind that he had fallen in love. He instinctively knew that Olivia would not only love Greece but his other large family too.

With his return flight looming in a matter of days he held Olivia against himself in her hotel bed, after another romantic yet sexy night of exploring and familiarizing himself with her voluptuous curves and her many erogenous zones, reveling in her unique sexual scent, and even her ticklish spots.

He had never enjoyed being with a woman so completely on all levels. As she softly sighed, her lovely leg resting over his lazy bones, he traced a slow finger over her arm.

"Are you hungry?"

"A little. But I don't want to move."

He chuckled, "I know what you mean. Let's have a shower, my delicious Olivia and then we can order room service." He heard himself purr and smiled in the dark.

She moaned, "Maybe later...much later. I'm too comfortable and soooo relaxed." He could hear her satisfied smile as she sighed into his shoulder. Pulling her even closer into himself, he kissed her temple and knew he would never forget her special aroma of fresh crushed gardenias and woman.

"I'm going to delay my flight back to next week."

Alex could make out her silhouette in the dimness. "As much as I'd like that you can't keep doing that."

"I suspected you'd say that. How about I fly you to Athens as soon as you're finished at the cottage?"

He felt her stiffen but continued holding her.

"If you're inviting me to visit you, I'll come, but I'm paying for myself."

"Okay, no need to be prickly about it. I meant nothing—"

"I know." She sighed and he could tell that she was trying to get herself back into that languid state of rest.

"You can stay in Athens for a few days and then we can drive to Porto Heli. You'll love it." As he whispered about the various things they could do and see there, her breathing slowed down and he was glad that she relaxed even more into him.

"I know. Sounds like a dream come true." He voice trailed off.

"I love you...*agápi mou.*" He whispered, his heart overflowing with emotions that felt so right and so perfect that it terrified him for a moment.

When he awoke Olivia's side of the bed was empty and his

heart constricted. He was thrown off by how much her absence disturbed him. The tension balling in his chest grew.

Hearing the shower running invited him to see if she needed an extra hand. She was still reticent in letting him see her fully naked in the morning, or even in the night light.

The thought of seeing those curves made him hard again. The thought of tantalizing her inner core with his tongue inflamed a more welcome tension in his body and mind.

Smiling he rose to join Olivia.

She squealed when she saw him and covered her breasts with her arms under the steaming hot water, and then laughed.

"Need a little help, my vixen?" As he joined her in the large shower stall he studied her wet face, slicked back red hair and gorgeous body under the steamy downpour, her arms slowly loosened and then reached out to him. He welcomed her into his arms.

He kissed her wet mouth, relishing the hot spray of the rain shower gushing over them both and his hands gravitated from her perfect hips up to her ample, divine breasts.

He admired her alabaster skin and marveled that the naked goddess appeared even more delectable than he had imagined. Even a decade ago, when their melding had happened in that large hotel linen closet, they had not seen each other naked. But he remembered these plump, perfect breasts. Excitement of the forbidden had escalated their need for each other. The memory of fresh lavender scented linens wafted into his mind even now. The scent of being happy, home, in Olivia's arms.

He couldn't have enough of those honey kisses as his hands explored and incited her pleasured moans.

He would never have enough of Olivia. He needed her again and watched the sinful delight and hunger deepen within her blue eyes as he imprisoned her against the warm, wet tiled wall. Raising her by her perfect derrière to better meld with her, as he entered her again her eyes closed.

This was what he had waited for.

Kneading his shoulder muscles and then wrapping her arms around his neck, Olivia kissed him and tightened her legs around his waist.

The growl from deep within him sounded strange, protective and feral as they both climbed to their shared heaven. Her breathless moans turned him on even more and he grabbed her mouth and continued plunging into her.

Picking her up fully still connected to one another, he sat on the bench behind them. The cool stone did nothing to lower the temperature of his intense desire. As Olivia leaned back against his upper thighs he held her as his tongue laved, teased and sucked at one breast and then . . . he stopped.

A diagonal red welt the size of a tooth pick adorned the outer side of her right breast.

She opened her eyes and froze.

"Oh. No," Alex heard himself say against the loudness of the steaming water.

He couldn't move.

"I had breast cancer three and a half years ago. But it's all fine now."

"The temporary illness which prevented you from coming to Maria and Sloan's wedding." He swallowed hard and despite the wet confined surroundings he couldn't breathe properly.

As his gaze switched from her breast to her eyes he saw Olivia's face paled.

Her eyes widened and she gasped at what she must have seen in his yes. She moved out of his arms and disconnected them from each other. Covering her breasts again with obviously trembling hands she seemed to shrivel inwards.

Standing up he stepped back from her.

She backed into the corner of the stall and then reached for the door.

He didn't stop her. Unable to breathe he had no clue what to do.

Images playing out inside his brain like a black and white film filled him with dread. Emotional clips of deep knowledge of a devastating loss in the distant past: A vision of a broken man whose tears racked his whole body as he kneeled by a large shimmering stone in the rain. Fear for not having a future and a forever together with the woman he loved. Seeing happiness snatched from them, Alex's emotions shut down.

CHAPTER 18

"I'm fed up with all the complaints about you treating the staff like rubbish." Costa, Alex's father said with a deep frown of his salt and pepper, bushy eyebrows above the green eyes his son had inherited.

Papa obviously did not appreciate being dragged back into the Athens office when Alex was supposed to have taken back the company reins upon his return. "You've been back nearly a month Alexo, and I won't stand for this anymore. Now tell me what's really going on. And don't bother saying it's not important, because I know my son and this is unlike you. You're like a miserable ghost. Like a bear with a sore tooth. Now talk." He set a glass with a shot of their favorite whiskey down with a little too much force in front of his son and waited.

After a few moments of silence Alex sighed, took the drink, emptied it and stared at his father. "It's a woman. She had breast cancer."

At his father's sharp intake of breath, Alex was mortified at feeling tears prickling the backs of his burning eyes and took off his glasses. He absently rubbed the bridge of his nose.

He hadn't slept for what felt like years.

112

Like a damned thief leaving Wrightsville Beach on the next available flight to Athens, he had just about made enough time to say goodbye to family members who were still there.

"She died? *Theé mou!*" My God, his father said, grabbing his son's shoulder with his large hand.

But Alex stared into space. "No. She had it a couple of years ago, but I didn't know and I was shocked. And then I blew it—again!"

Now, facing the rest of his life in his self-inflicted hell he couldn't blame his father and those around him for their impatience with him. He squeezed his tear-filled eyes shut expecting his father to tell him what he already knew.

He was a fool, *Touvlo!*

Instead he opened his eyes and saw his father sit next to him. Donning his glasses he tried to compose himself and waited. Because he still couldn't find a way forward, feeling like a man lost in space with no way back.

Sighing again his father shook his head. "Ah, my son, don't be so hard on yourself. This makes much sense, now. What will you do?"

Watching his father's ruddy complexion, Alex shrugged. "I hurt Olivia too much. There's nothing to be—"

"There's always something you can do, Alexo. It's there in your name, in your DNA."

"I'm not like you, Papa. I'm not like my other brothers, either. I may know business, but love. . ." He shook his head, no longer embarrassed of showing his emotions.

"Well, at least *there's* a first. I've never heard you say anything about love before." His father's smile brightened.

"I'm not as strong as you, Papa. I couldn't bear to lose Olivia. Not after losing Mama to the same disease. I may have not have remembered her or what she went through, but I know too well what it did to you. I remember standing with you by her graveside..." He remembered those visits to a strange and eerie place with large stones where he had seen his father break down again and again. It had taken years after living away with the Andersons for those nightmares to stop. Over the following years after Sandra and Jason and later Aunt Jenny had explained to him about death and that yes, his mother was in heaven and not coming back, had he started putting things together in his mind.

When Alex's eyes blurred and overflowed with more tears he wiped them from behind his glasses and no longer cared if he was a wimp in addition to being a cowardly idiot.

Alex answered Papa's questions and then his father shook his head, "So you threw it all away *now*? You know deep inside that love even for a few short years is better than not having it at all. And this woman is obviously one of the lucky ones to have survived it. These days it's different, Alexo, much can be done to diagnose cancer early and take care of it with a very high rate of full recovery. Or is there more to this than meets the eye?"

"No, Papa, everything else was working out perfectly. I just screwed it up with the only woman I'll ever love.

After a pause, Papa asked, "Have you spoken to your mother? Sandra must have had something to say about all this."

This time Alex shook his head, avoiding his father's astute eyes. "I haven't spoken to her. I couldn't stay!" Alex shut his eyes at the deep shame that filled him.

"Right. Enough of feeling sorry for yourself, Alexo, and no more excuses. You know what you need to do." Squeezing his son's upper arm he emphasized, "Immediately."

~

"Mom, please don't give me a hard time, you can't possibly say anything that I don't already know about myself. I've come for your help. I've royally screwed up." Alex said firmly after explaining everything his mother needed to know.

"Calm down, Alex, my poor boy." She gently cupped his face within her palms, studying him. "All this weight that you've lost and those bags under your beautiful eyes tell me that you've beaten yourself up plenty already. And I'm sure it's not all that unsalvageable. You've always been too hard on yourself."

"You met Olivia, you could see what a lovely person she is and you can't tell me that I've got any chance in hell to getting her to even listen to my apology, never mind giving me yet another chance."

She put in front of him a plate of his favorite bolognaise dish with extra grated parmesan cheese. "First you eat, then you get some sleep and then we'll sort all this out."

The hope he had harbored all the way back to Wrightsville Beach now almost disintegrated at the sight of Olivia's favorite dish. This time he was going to get a grip and stop letting tears come whenever they felt like it. What was next? Him having periods and crying into a large tub of ice-cream like a besotted teenage girl!

You're a man, damn it, man up!

"Maria promised not to divulge Olivia's whereabouts, and she's back home in Arlington in two weeks. I need to see her as soon as possible. She'll never return my calls. And who can blame her? I need to see Olivia face to face right now, damn it."

"I know. Sit. We'll get there, together. You're a very smart guy and I have every faith that just like the rest of your brothers, you'll get your happy-ever-after too, and soon. Love will find a way, you'll see." Mom reassured him like she had when he was little, when he had tried and failed to stop his brothers babying him or goading him as they were growing up.

She kissed his forehead, "After your nap you're going for a boat ride with Dad. It'll be nice for both of you to catch up. I'm just glad you've come to your senses. I knew the moment I saw you both together that you were meant to be together. And

Olivia's worth the fight. Now eat." She smiled and he reluctantly picked up his cutlery.

~

"I don't know where you can meet Olivia. And frankly, I don't want you anywhere near her, Alexander." Maria said, her unwavering stare telling him much more than her softly spoken words. Then she eyed her toddler as Tyler concentrated on his favorite treasure board game. "You hurt my best friend. You treated her worse than her ex did when she needed him the most. He actually walked out on her the day before the first surgery. But that didn't knock her out like you did. You know why that is? Because she fell in love with you. I think she always loved you, you fool."

"I'm the biggest ass. I know that better than anyone. But please trust me, Maria. I have to see Olivia. I need her. I've never thought—never mind said—sappy crap like, 'she's my destiny,' but now I know Olivia *is* my life." He didn't care that he sounded desperate. "I've come to my senses, and although I may be too late, I want to see her one last time. To apologize at least."

Maria shook her head. The pause stretched unbearably, but then some of the gentleness in her eyes returned as she tilted her head in thought, relinquished her heavy bundle of joy into Alex's arms and said, "You can toss a ball with your oldest nephew and earn your uncledom."

Then as he waited for the smallest morsel of mercy, she rolled her blue eyes at him and sighed. "Don't give me that lost-puppy-dog look, Alex. I don't know how you can see her because I can't tell you that your mother bought me and Olivia a special gift of a relaxing day at the spa this Friday. Neither can I tell you that I'll be at the Grand Queen Anne spa from 11am in…" She recited the address as if it was of no importance.

It was an hour's drive away but Alex would have driven across the country right now just to see Olivia. He knew from the enchanted days—*who talks like that, you besotted fool!*—getting to know Olivia, that the best friends had a standing arrangement, spending some pampering time together once a month, no matter how busy their lives got.

"The massage therapist Elke *may* be open to my best friend's romance story once I tell her all about it. And she *may* leave Olivia alone in a certain room at a certain time." She arched her brows and stared into his eyes. "If you ever pull another stunt like that again I'll feed you to the wolves—don't worry, I'll find some."

He leaned in and kissed her forehead. "Sloan sure chooses good wives." He felt the first smile in weeks somewhat relax his facial muscles as he held his nephew up in the air. Tyler laughed at being an airborne plane and Alex breathed a little easier knowing that he would see his love soon.

"Less of the charm, you're still in deep, deep trouble."

"There isn't a chance that I could see Olivia sooner, like right now?"

"Don't push it. And I can't guarantee that Olivia won't send you packing. I wouldn't blame her one bit if she does." Maria gave him a stern penetrating stare she must have learned from Sloan, and turned away from him. "Now earn your keep and make up for your absence in the past few weeks. Tyler's missed you. And for goodness' sake eat something, you look haunted and hungry."

"It's a new diet called 'eating crow'." For the first time in ages Alex felt a little more alive and hopeful.

CHAPTER 19

The soothing soft music washed over Olivia as she lay on her tummy on the massage table and slowly breathed in and out through the opening of its pillowy head rest. The healing scent of lavender, eucalyptus and something delicious wrapped her with surprising inner calm.

Within the quiet music, the gentle swelling and ebbing of the ocean lapping the imaginary shore was so evocative she had to stop herself reverting to the melancholy of the past long weeks.

She wouldn't think about Alexander's masculine scent, his touch or his charm. Or reminisce about her many talks about Greece with him over their shared weeks together.

She ached with need for him, yearning to be there—with him.

But it was a futile waste of energy and tears. He had hurt her too much.

She didn't need any man and resolved to get a cat—her sister Lisa would adore that—and live out her life following in Aunt Jenny's footsteps. She would lavish her love and adoration on Maria's and Gemma's children and that would have to suffice.

How she would go back to Wrightsville Beach she didn't know yet, but she was made of strong stuff. Admittedly she had been unable to stay at Aunt Jenny's almost completely finished beach house, after the coward had flown out of her hotel room like the proverbial bat out of hell over five long weeks ago.

Maria had understood and insisted that Olivia accept the new project close enough to her home in Arlington, and had said she would take care of the rest of the finishing touches at the cottage.

Whether Maria had put it up on the market or not Olivia didn't want to hear anything about it. It held too many memories all joined by the adult romance that Alexander had rekindled with his determination and charm.

She sighed and refused to think about anything other than the here and now and surrendering to the pampering hours in her favorite spa.

Hearing a soft shuffle she didn't open her eyes. The power of her thoughts and her relaxed state actually evoked that wonderful distinctive scent that was uniquely Alexander's. Like the Greek sun, exotic flowers and flaky baked pastries all rolled into one sexy package.

When warm hands gently touched her hair, she determined to make the most of Maria's and her mother-in-law's timely and welcome gift. Her two friends were lucky to have Sandra as their no-nonsense but loving mother-in-law.

The massage therapist's large hands were firm, but so soothing and wreaking such pleasure that she was glad she had capitulated to Maria's demands to join her today.

She fell deeper into the Zen mood. When she sighed a small deep groan above her roused her from her reverie.

Had she just felt a slight overlap of knowing fingers near the outer sides of her breasts? Or was she losing her mind?

Heart beating too fast she raised her heavy head slightly to her left to get a glimpse of her therapist.

At the instant recognition, she nearly fell off the high table and Alexander caught her as if expecting her reaction.

"What the *hell*!" She squealed.

Pushing herself out of his arms she wriggled off the massage table, dragging the sheet around her. "How did you get in here? No, Maria…How d-dare you t-touch me?"

Staring up at him while fastening the sheet across her torso she tried to cover as much of herself as possible. She didn't care about the heat over her face and neck. And she told her betraying heart to just stop thumping like that.

Just collect yourself and breathe.

"I needed to see you, Olivia. Please listen just for one moment." Alexander appeared so different, much taller and leaner, and—

What did she care about what he looked like? He devastated her whole life, he broke her heart *again*!

"For your sake I'd better be dreaming." She gritted her teeth. "Because no way can you seriously be standing here in front of me. You…" She had never sworn but she was so tempted to swear right now.

"Olivia, I'm so sorry. If you just give—"

"Oh, no, I will not listen to you. Not now, not ever." Every word threatened her breathing and tears shed over her cheeks. "Not only did you break my heart a second time and I let you, you took me to meet your whole family and let me imagine a future with you. You're a self-centered pig for coming here and re-digging everything up again."

Alexander weaved his way around the massage table and stood too close to her. "Please, Olivia, I was such damn fool, I was taken by surprise. I was in shock. I'm so sorry to have hurt—"

"Get away from me, you coward. You insensitive brute." She sniveled and as he tried to touch her the anger surging within her over the past weeks exploded.

She took in a deep painful breath and before she realized her own intent she slapped him across the face. Once, twice and again as Alexander stood where he was, with a stoic expression.

It didn't help her feel better or different at all.

She screamed.

His immobility fanned her fury: As if giving her the opportunity to get her anger and frustration out of her system. His body stance, his downturned chin and those green eyes all told that he deserved her inflicting so much more pain than she was trying to cause him.

Suddenly spent, her heart pounding too much, unable to breath she lowered her head, about to sink onto the ground.

She felt Alexander's strong arms swoop her up, pulling her into himself, against his chest. He held her so protectively, so tightly that she could hear the heavy thud of his heart against her ear.

He smelled so damn good that she cried even more. "I fell for you... I gave my all to you, just like the first time....How could you leave me like that?" She hiccupped, not caring about her tears wetting the front of his shirt.

He repeated softly, "I'm so sorry, Olivia, *agápi mou*," until she pulled away from him.

Although he wouldn't release her out of his grasp at least she saw his face.

The tears in his eyes stopped her for a moment.

"It's a pathetic explanation now that I've had time to think about it all, but my biological mother died of breast cancer when I was three. When I saw your scar, all I could think of was how devastated my father and my family were at losing her... But it's inexcusable, unforgivable, how much I hurt you, *agápi mou*."

She felt her lower lip tremble, needing to touch that beloved gorgeous face and those silky black curls now once again overgrown and falling over his forehead and temples. But she stopped herself and instead reinforced her heart with facts and reminders of never giving anyone a second or third chance to annihilate her ever again.

She would no longer get sucked into his orbit of charm and need and even love.

"Did you think I had any choice in getting the cancer? No, you didn't think of me. Look at yourself, the way you just winced." Her vision blurred, the tightness in her chest squeezing even harder now. She looked away from him, trying to pull out of his arms.

But he still wouldn't let her out of his vice grip.

"No, that's not it at all... I'm so sorry, Olivia. My heart hurts so much for what you've gone through, for what I've put you through. You're so giving and so generous I wish you hadn't suffered at all. Please forgive me. I truly love and adore you. Please let me make it all up to you. I need—"

His words escalated her tension and she pushed at him. This time he freed her immediately and scanned her face as if gauging her ability to stand on her own two feet.

Hell yeah, she could and she would.

"There are no more chances, Alexander. I've had enough of being manipulated and then rejected so cruelly. I'm sorry you lost your mother so young. But you can never make up for this. You still have a large family in your life...Why am I even talking to you? I may have been brought up to be more forgiving and being more like Aunt Jenny, but no more—"

"Aunt Jenny brought us together—"

She interrupted his earnest words, "Don't you dare talk about her. Just stop. It's too late."

"No, it's never too—"

"Go." Unable to bear the sight of him, yet another part of her breaking heart died all over again.

His desperation, his helplessness only proved how over-whelmed he still was. Was his ego still pushing him even now to work this out? Had his determination to succeed at romance pushed him to return here?

She could see how overwhelmed he was.

With a steadying breath she said, "Look, I don't blame you for anything, Alexander. I should have known from our past that you're not the committing type. And now I understand why, hearing about your mother. Maybe you'll never be ready for real love. It's not your fault. But I deserve better. Truly loving someone means that you'll do anything for them, especially in times of need or crisis. Love is about being there at all times and not just when it's working or it's fun and romantic. And I don't need anyone anymore, least of all, *you.*"

He seemed to step back for a moment. But she calmly continued. Looking straight into his eyes she said, "Thank you for apologizing. I needed the closure. We both need closure and to move on."

The panic or was it rage that sparked in those green eyes made her stop.

"Closure! No way. I'm here to do whatever it takes to earn your trust, Olivia. Once and for all, and this time I'm not leaving you. I realized that I couldn't bear the thought of losing you, and instead I hurt us both. My life is meaningless without you. I'll be there for you no matter what. Just like you've been there for me, willing to help me even with my stupid convoluted plans because I didn't have the guts to just ask for what I really wanted…just you. It's always been you. I'm serious, Olivia. *Agápi mou—*"

She sighed, shook her head and forced herself to add, "You've said what you need to say, now it's finished, that soft and forgiving Olivia is gone forever." She could no longer look into those beautiful, hurting eyes. It felt like she was jabbing a knife into herself when she saw that pain.

The silence was charged with too much emotion. Minutes seemed to seep by and still not looking up at him she said, "Just leave or this time I will."

After a long sigh he said, "I wish you only love and happiness, Olivia." He then strode towards the door, opened it and finally left her alone.

Only then did she allow herself to crumble to the carpeted

floor until long moments passed and Maria was holding her tightly.

~

Olivia was one hundred percent right. Alex was nothing like his brothers. Even Grey had regarded him with disappointment last night when saying goodbye again.

"Grey, don't say what I can read in your eyes, damn it. I know it's almost a life-long habit of me running. Leaving and justifying it all in the name of growing up, progress, business…anything to avoid admitting the truth."

He was no Greek warrior, he was just a fool. Only this time it had cost him everything.

"Well, in business you run towards challenges, the bigger and more insurmountable the more you like it. So don't give me the sob story. We all know what you're capable of in all other aspects of your life. So you're a bit obtuse where love is concerned, there's still hope for you."

"No, Grey, I've lost Olivia forever. How can I blame her? Would Mom have turned away from Dad when he had to have urgent heart surgery a few years back? Mom and Dad are always there for all us all and always have been."

I, on the other hand am a disgrace to both my families.

Too little, too late.

"I know a bit about Olivia and from what I hear she's the kind who just needs some time to process this."

"Not this time. I know I did my very best but there's literally nothing else I can do…apart from kidnapping her and dragging her to Greece. I've hurt her too deeply and too often."

"Why had I concocted that stupid plan to get her help to win over another woman? She's a saint, for God's sake. And when she had given me another chance what did I do? Added more emotional scars on top of her own. I don't deserve Olivia, and now she finally had had enough of me."

Grey took another swig at his beer and listened then said, "I still stand by my advice to give her time."

The vivid image of the pain in those bruised eyes had been his undoing.

Touvlo, you made your bed, now die in it.

Now, thousands of feet up in the air, Alex didn't care if the plane taking him back to Greece ever landed there. Why bother to live if it meant living without his true love?

He had taken the leap of faith, had listened to his loved ones' advice, had bared his soul to Olivia, had been transparent about his feelings to her, and it had all come to nothing.

She had called it closure, like the final nail on the coffin, and all the other cliché phrases which now made sense.

He was lost and homeless without Olivia.

CHAPTER 20

The nightmare was the same almost every night; Olivia was strolling alongside Alexander on a perfect, cobalt blue seashore with Greek churches in the sun drenched vista, and when she ran from him he seemed to be drowning in misery without her.

The other dreams in which they were running, laughing, making love, awoke her to even deeper depression.

No matter how exhausted Olivia was by the end of her long, busy days on her latest project only forty minutes drive away from home in Arlington she felt even more tired with each day. This redesign assignment was nowhere near as much fun or as creative as Aunt Jenny's beach house had been, but it was many miles away from all the memories of her summer fling.

Don't kid yourself, she grumbled as her heart refused to settle to its lethargic, irregular beat.

The dreams always dragged her back into that gorgeous, bright and airy beach house that some other family would soon enjoy. Everywhere, in every corner she had seen a little of Alexander's suggestions and decisions they had taken together, playing house.

So it was absolutely fine with her never to see it again. After those kisses and romantic times spent in Alexander's arms in various parts of the house and in back yard, she never wanted to go anywhere near that part of the beach. If her best friend didn't live in Wrightsville Beach she would have avoided the whole place, too.

She was still working on ridding herself of the memories of the haze of the pain surrounding her on those last days after Alexander had bailed on her. Even when she had returned home wherever she went her memories followed her like heavy, cold, torrential clouds in those cartoons and commercials selling depression medication.

Olivia focused on letting go of her naive romantic notions and knew she had to move on.

She had to learn to be pragmatic and realistic about the difference between dreams and wishful thinking. And romantic stories in movies and books, as opposed to real life. That despite what a man thought he wanted, he just wasn't capable to giving anyone what he didn't possess inside.

Since seeing Alexander two weeks ago she still couldn't stop thinking and dreaming about him. The closure should have helped them both, damn it.

But something wasn't sitting right within her.

She had to do something, but what?

Now driving to Wrightsville Beach to visit Maria, and later spend some time with Gemma, too, Olivia needed to have a heart to heart with her trusted friend. She was completely out of her element as to how to move forward and knew that Maria would listen and understand.

Even if Maria couldn't help, at least Olivia could vent or do something to escape this life in limbo.

Whenever Maria called her over the past few weeks it hurt to hear Tyler in the background, imagining Alexander giving someone else gorgeous dark-haired children. The memory of how nurturing he had been with Gemma and Grey's baby Jordan blurred her vision even now.

She shook her head and forced herself to stop this self-pity. She had gone through worse when losing her loved ones. And although seeing Alexander again had totally thrown her off track, that part of her life was now firmly in the past.

She was strong and would find a way to get on with her life.

For all she knew, Alexander may have already replaced her with someone else. The vision incited such jealousy she shoved the thought out of her mind and concentrated on the road ahead.

This too shall pass, as Aunt Jenny used to say whenever Olivia had confided in her about her uttermost secrets. She missed her so much she stopped thinking about her mentor whom she had loved almost as much as her own parents.

As she settled into Maria's kitchen chair, hugging a down-filled cushion against her trembling tummy she opened up to her friend about her confusing thoughts. If sadness overwhelmed her she allowed herself to go there. When tears came she let them. Maria listened to her and hugged her, while watching over her two-year-old Tyler sucking on a toast soldier in his high chair.

Olivia was grateful that Sloan was out for most of the day with Wyatt and Logan, who were still visiting the family, enjoying the beautiful last weeks of summer.

"I don't blame you one bit to feel this conflicted, Liv. I know that feeling too well when Sloan...." Maria stopped and stared at her friend.

Olivia shook her head, "But this is different. Sloan loves you and you worked it through."

"Alexander loves you, too. Much more than even he realizes. He came to you, didn't he? I saw how you were both affected by seeing each other. I believe you're soul mates." Maria brought up a hand, "Let me finish, Liv. I understand you were taken by surprise to see him at the spa, and it devastated you. But you agree that it took him a lot of courage to see you. Now that you've had a couple of weeks to ruminate, don't you feel a *little* bit different?"

Olivia almost squirmed at the question. "I don't want to still care for him. I *will* find a way forward, to leave all this…despair behind. Love shouldn't hurt so much. We're better off not hurting each other anymore. And I asked him that whenever we see each other at any occasions we'll both just have to deal with it civilly." She swallowed the lump down her constricting throat.

"So you don't feel like a big part of you is missing." Maria's expression told Olivia that she saw through her bravado.

"I can't go on like this. I'll get over him, we'll both move on."

"My gut says that you both still have unfinished business. And I have something for you from Grandma Jenny." That same excited sparkle in her friend's eyes made Olivia's heart beat faster.

A few minutes later Maria returned with a white envelope and handed it to her. "Grandma stipulated that I give you this when you were ready. Knowing her, I'm sure it'll help you understand Alexander better. I should have told you about his past when you met again this summer, but I didn't know he'd react like that…I should have predicted that even though he was only three when he lost his mom, witnessing his father going through hell must have totally screwed him up. And he's still been dealing with it all. Maybe after reading this you'll even consider calling him or even…"

"Why would you think I should forgive him?" Olivia asked despite the fluttering hope blossoming within her.

"Because that's who you are, and you know who Alexander is inside. *And*…you love each other. It's obvious to us all that he's your one and only, Liv. The time has come for you to take a leap of faith one more time and give the poor guy a chance. He's bereft without you."

Maria gave her a steady look and then smiled at Tyler who now clutched within his fist his own spoon for his favorite chocolate pudding, focusing on aiming a dollop into his open mouth as if it was a matter of 'do or die'.

Maria's eyes shone as she looked back at Olivia, "I hope the letter helps. I waited until you'd recovered enough and were ready to undertake and enjoy the renovation project. Once you started, I thought it was a perfect opportunity for you to finally revisit your first love. I've waited a long time for you guys to have your own happy-ever-after. And the moment I saw you both together I knew that all along Grandma had been right about you belonging together."

Olivia's goose-bumps covered her whole body, in delicious reawakening waves. "So Aunt Jenny *had* sent Alexander so we could meet and work together on the gala fundraiser?"

"Yup, she sure did." Maria's smile brightened further as she cleaned up Tyler's face and took his messy bib off. "Now while I put this big boy down for his nap, you read the letter and then do what you know you've got to do. Alexander can't help being a guy." She chuckled, maneuvering her little boy towards Olivia as if knowing her friend couldn't resist kissing her god son.

Olivia sniffed at the adorable boy's talcum-scented head, kissed him and then hugged him.

"We've got to give them some time to grow up, Liv. Now say bye-bye to your aunt Olivia, Tyler."

"Olee-veeaa, play, Olee...veeaa" Tyler repeated again trying to squirm out of his mother's arms. "Play, now."

"Maybe after your nap but right now, let's go and have a short nap, otherwise we'll have a grumpy Tyler instead of the sweet one." Maria tickled under his arm and he started to giggle.

Hearing his name uttered by the adored little master the big dog Ollie picked up his head from his sleeping quarters and was instantly on duty. The mutt's large brown eyes focused on the toddler in his mother's arms and Ollie's nails clicked a fast rhythmic tap as he followed mother and toddler out of the kitchen. His large tail knocked over Tyler's wooden block set structure on the way.

Staring at the letter in her hands Olivia couldn't—didn't want to—delay the inevitable. Her hands trembled and her heart did all sorts of summersaults within her chest as she ripped open one side of the envelope.

My darling Olivia,

If you're receiving this letter then unfortunately it means you and Alexander have still not made your way fully into love, and to each other.

I know everyone always called me a romantic fool, but nothing is more important than love. And I leave you with the gift of knowledge that all roads do, indeed lead to love.

If you and Alexander are still trying to find your way forward together then I hope that you've learned about his background by now.

I share here what I learned through the years of knowing the Andersons and what I pieced together about Alexander's unfortunate situation from Sandra when the boys were still quite young.

When he was a teenager Sandra had confided in me that she wished she knew how to help Alexander learn to trust his own instincts about love, instead of pushing away anyone he felt strongly about. It had taken Sandra and Jason constant reassurance that he was not alone and that he was loved just as much as the rest of the boys.

It also seemed to help him immensely when his biological father came back for him when he turned thirteen. By then Alexander had stopped having nightmares and felt like he truly was part of the Anderson clan. We'd talked about his having the best of both worlds, here and in his birth country.

All those summers spent with his father and the large family in Greece had strengthened him, but not enough to go with the flow when he met and fell in love with you.

He was twenty but he still fought his demons, putting up all sorts of barriers around himself.

We used to have long philosophical discussions about life and the universe and I realized just how vulnerable he felt despite all the love around him. I saw some breakthroughs when we discussed the less fortunate people in the world. And I was gratified and proud of how he gave of himself so easily and generously to good causes and to the needy —so much like you, my lovely Olivia.

Sandra once hugged me and said, "You're a gift to us all, and especially to Alexander. You get through to him like no one else seems capable. It's because of you that he's started to help others and appreciate how lucky he truly is."

I was so glad that in my own way I could help.

Therapy also helped him to a certain extent but when he fell so deeply in love with you I saw clearly how afraid he was to love you, to be vulnerable and to risk losing....

So obviously he decided to turn away from any pain and concentrate all his attention on his family and his business.

I wish I could be there for you both, but if you're receiving this letter then it means there's still some ways to go for your love to find its own course.

The young man I knew and loved was as stubborn and proud as he was determined to conquer his fears.

Is he still fighting them, or has he worked on it but still pushed love away? Is he still placing obstacles in his own way?

*O*livia's heart thumped so hard as she devoured the handwritten words in Aunt Jenny's perfect, flowery script. How well she had known the boy, and how sad that the boy had not really grown as much as he could have. Or had he?

Hadn't Alexander sought her out? Hadn't he looked like a suffering mess, like she felt inside, too?

Her eyes scanned the next paragraph as she tried to steady her fingers and focus.

efore he left for Greece on the day of the gala he came to me and confided that he had expected the two of you to go together, but you had agreed to go with Brad.

I knew something wasn't right but I also saw he was running scared. That instead of asking you about it he needed to escape. He still wasn't ready for you, for love.

When I asked him if he'd spoken to you about it he was adamant that the two of you had been 'a mistake' and that it was for the best that he permanently return to Greece, to his reality.

That he belonged there with his biological family.

I could see he was hurting but also knew that he needed more time to grow up, to grow resilient, to experience life, and to learn to appreciate true love.

Maybe you both did...You were both so young.

Sandra also saw what her son was doing but she set him free to find his own path in his own time.

I hope now fate has brought you both the opportunity to let love blossom.

Be patient with Alexander. He's the rare kind of man who once he commits to a woman he will love her forever. But his pride or fear may get in the way.

Do what you need to do, but do not give up on Alexander.

I have loved you both from the start and as the romantic soul, I bid you love and joy together, forever.

ears streamed down Olivia's face, but the beginnings of a tiny trembling smile tugged at her lips. She reread the letter again.

As many thoughts whirred through her mind, something deep

within her reawakened. Just like whenever she had been with Alexander.

Among the butterflies within her chest she knew a feeling of certainty which had eluded her for too long.

She had to see Alexander.

Her place was with Alexander.

He had taken big strides towards growing up by having orchestrated a meeting with her at the spa, despite her determination to avoid him at all costs. He had laid it all on the line.

He was finally being as straight forward and honest with her as he was in his business dealings. Was he finally ready to risk himself for love?

It seemed her dream of visiting Greece was about to become a reality.

CHAPTER 21

Olivia didn't bother knocking, but grasped the large brass door knob with her slightly clammy palm. Through the glass of the big wall panels and doors, with his back to his desk and to her, she saw the imposing Alexander standing by the huge windows, watching the sprawling smog-ridden skyline of hot Athens.

Opening the door she took in a fortifying breath, held it and then slowly exhaled. "I'm searching for the guide who'd offered to show me around the city and the islands."

At her first words, Alexander spun around to face her. The pleasure on his beaming face made her ache inside. She had missed this damned fool for too long, until she couldn't bear to live one more day without seeing him.

How right it had felt after spending last weekend with Maria, to make arrangements to book the soonest flight to Athens.

As if realizing too late that he had shown his true feelings Alexander strode the few steps to his desk, his face devoid of any emotion and asked, "What makes you think the guide's still available and interested?"

"I remember someone telling me once that it's never too late.

Is it too late, Alexander?" Olivia arched her brows as she sauntered closer to him with the desk between them. "Of course, the world's my oyster and I could get another guide to show me . . . around beautiful Greece."

The smirk he was obviously trying to repress surfaced as he strode around the desk to stand before her. "Like hell you will, you vixen." Putting his arms around her he swept her up off the ground. As he scanned her face he grinned, "So you came to your senses and have forgiven this idiot."

"Well," Olivia stretched the word, but as he studied her face, her eyes and then finally stopped at her mouth she forgot everything else.

Their lips met in sweet hunger as if magnetically charged for each other. They kissed long and hard, and all her tiredness of the many long hours spent in transit disintegrated.

Slowly he let her feet touch the floor, but didn't release her. "I can't believe you're here, in my arms." He kissed her temple and sighed deeply as if finally able to breathe properly.

Just then a knock at the door was followed by an older version of Alexander entering the room.

"Oh, I'm sorry..." As the man registered the situation, his smile broadened as he came in.

Keeping one arm around her Alexander introduced her, "Olivia, this is my father, Costa Kyriakou. Papa, this is Olivia."

She shook the older man's proffered hand feeling her whole body move with the heartfelt handshake. Then she was swallowed up in a big hug by the stocky man with grey hair and darker mustache.

"I am very happy to make your acquaintance, and welcome to Greece! Now I'll leave you two, as I'm sure you have some catching up to do."

"Nice to meet you too, Mr. Kyriakou."

"Please, call me Costa." He smiled as he retreated towards the door after the unmistakable, meaningful glance between father and son.

As soon as they were alone, Alexander reached for a remote and with a press of a button the wall of glass and the door were covered with cream blinds.

Then he swept her up into his arms. "Yes, we have a lot of catching up to do. I love you, Olivia and I'll prove that every day for the rest of my life, if indeed you're here to give me another chance."

Olivia flicked her hair back behind her shoulders and reached out to hold his beloved face within her palms.

How she had missed him. "No more self reprimanding, Alexander. I'm sorry it took me some time to recognize the truth, that I love you just the way you are. And that we belong together. We'll make it all work. And if you get any ideas of running anywhere out of my sight I'll duct tape you to the bed. You've been warned." For the first time she felt the pure joy without any shadow of the past or fear for the future which was mirrored in his eyes.

"Say that again."

"Which part? Is your dirty mind finding innuendoes?"

"That too, we'll revisit that in a moment. But the part where you love me."

Through her happy tears she watched the boyish excitement in those green eyes as he waited.

"I love you, always have, Alexander." She welcomed another bear hug from her love. "And I know now what you meant about Aunt Jenny. I should have known she'd tried to set us up all those years ago. Wasn't she something?" She marveled.

"She knew we were meant to be together, but I wasn't mature or strong enough back then."

She stared up at his face, "You look so good, Alexander, I've missed you so, so much." She weaved her hungry fingers through his dense, curly hair, bringing his head closer so she could kiss him again. "Looks like you need another trim, unless you don't want me to boss you around."

"I welcome any of your bossing at any time, forever. Just be patient with me and help me along the way, so I don't screw up again." As she nodded he added, "To make up for the lost time, what would you say about us taking a long boat trip around the islands together? Then we can spend an uninterrupted week at the beach house?"

"That sounds perfect, but if you're talking about Aunt Jenny's cottage, we'll have to make sure with Maria about staying there first."

"Why? Didn't she tell you that it's ours?"

"What did you say?" Had she misheard?

"Maria has gifted the house to us both. She said that that's what her grandmother would have wanted. But I thought I'd blown it all forever."

"Oh my God!" She shook her head, feeling dizzy and breathless at the news. "The beach house is ours?" So much made sense now. "So that's why both you and Maria had encouraged me to put my own personal tastes into the place. Why she'd waited for me to renovate it with her. And you knew all along and that's why you also made suggestions..."

"I'm so glad you love it as much as I do." He swooped her up and spun her round, making her laugh. A true joyous laugh from deep within her.

"It's perfect. How could I not when there's so much of both of us in that place?"

As it all registered, that all this was going to work out after all, that their love did find its way at last, Olivia hugged him tighter. If she weren't so elated to be in Alexander's arms she would have cried.

But no more tears. Ever.

As he kissed her this time the urgency turned soft and explorative... then playful. He groaned and with a blooming grin he scanned her face, "Now, I'd like to revisit that visual about duct taping me to the bed. I can't wait till we get back to my place…"

"I can see a sofa but…on the other hand your desk looks very tempting…" She didn't hide her own state of increasing anticipation. "And I've always fantasized of having a corporate fling."

"Well, let me not stand in the way of a fantasy that I'm all too willing to take part in." As he picked her up in his arms and gently sat her down on the empty corner of his desk, his hands reacquainted themselves with her curves. And she welcomed the growing heat in his eyes which burned right into her heart. Any of her remaining reservations melted away as he pressed another button and she heard a latch click at the door.

She turned from him and with her hands poised above the leather accessories, shiny thick pens and neat piles of papers, she waited for his agreement.

When he nodded she pushed away everything off the large antique desk. The dramatic clatter added to her excitement as he swiveled her back to face him, "I've always wanted to do—"

She never finished the sentence as his mouth swooped on top of hers and they were lost in each other's arms.

~

*W*ith the afternoon sun peering through the smog filled skies overlooking the Acropolis views, Olivia couldn't believe that she was here ensconced in Alexander's protective, loving arms.

They had moved their second love making session to the more comfortable sofa and now they lay spent and sated under the soft pale blue pashmina throw.

Alexander was trailing a lazy thumb over her wrist and hand as she drowsily smiled into that wonderful face of her beloved. "It's a dream come true. You're my dream come true, Alexander. I want to fill our lives with laughter and lots of children and family gatherings."

He nodded, obviously speechless for a moment. Then he grinned and said, "Sounds heavenly. Marry me, Olivia. Immediately." Then his smile broadened. "Just so that Mom and the rest of the family lay off me now that the last son will also be happily married!"

She loved that twinkle in those green eyes. "Yes, I'll marry you just for that. But we'll plan it a bit, if that's okay with you. Perhaps have the ceremony at the Anderson estate overlooking the beach."

His smile grew wider. "You're one generous woman, Olivia. And then where would you like to honeymoon, and where would you like to live?"

"Let's have the best of both worlds, Alexander. As long as we're together. That's all that will ever matter to me."

He nodded and after another long kiss he studied her face again. "I hope you'll always look at me the way you see me now. Outside of business, I only cared about what I looked like when I saw myself through your eyes."

"And *you* make me feel perfect just the way I am."

"Because you are perfect, Olivia. You've always been perfect."

GLORIA SILK'S BOOKS

Do you believe in love at first sight?

First love has never been more intense, heartbreaking, and oh so worth it!

Shy artist Lia cannot resist gorgeous genius, Devraj. One rain soaked kiss changes the landscape of both their lives forever as sparks fly and their families and friends try to break them apart. Will Lia's loyalty to her cultural ties force her to forsake her forbidden love or can she stand up for her first and only love and face their uncharted future head on?

Amazon ASIN: B00N7VTCE4 iBooks Nook KOBO Google Play Google Books

Debut novel, First and Only Destiny

"Beautifully written love story with a perfect happy ever after. The prose in this book is extraordinary, the emotions heart-breaking and the author leaves you hanging on the edge right to the end of the story..." **Elizabeth Lennox**, Author of the Thorpe Brothers series

WHAT CAME NEXT**?**

In the end of *First and Only Destiny* Lia and Devraj finally got their well-deserved Happily Ever After!

BUT! Then I wondered what if instead of living the rest of their lives together in bliss they were torn apart?

So I wrote **Second Destiny** where almost twenty years later Lia is a mother of two and married. On the day Lia realizes she cannot stay in her loveless marriage to the 'right' Jewish man chosen by her grandparents decades earlier, Devraj is at her door trying to protect his nephew and Lia's 18 year-old daughter from repeating their own star-crossed love affair?

Well, read SECOND DESTINY now! BUY SECOND DESTINY

Years ago, the older generation broke Lia and Devraj apart. Now, the younger generation reunites them.

Lia's world turns upside down again when minutes after she demands a divorce from her cheating husband, Devraj is at her door. Will Lia again choose duty over the desires of her heart?

BUY NOW: Amazon ASIN: B00N7YI3CI iBooks Nook Kobo Google Play Google Books

∽

NOBODY'S BABY BUT MINE Available April 28, 2018

"Gripping, sensuous and astute."

Can Rachel and James find their way back into each other's hearts after tasting temptation and facing devastating news? How strong is love in the face of reality?

Order Now: **Amazon ASIN: B0782LB71J – iBooks   Nook   Kobo Google Play   Google Books**

∽

Summer, 2018: Healing Love - After beautiful young artist's craving for love endangers her restaurant business and her life she resolves to get help. How can she turn her life around and find everlasting love if her nightmares keep recurring?

ABOUT GLORIA SILK

Ever since Gloria Silk was little her passion was creating and sharing her romantic stories with others. She always loved reading contemporary and historical novels that grasped her imagination. Gloria now writes intense, sensuous love stories with happy endings.

In addition to writing romance and women's fiction, she enjoys writing intercultural romances and about family bonds. What can be more important in life than love and family?

Born in Russia, Gloria Silk has visited and lived in amazing, exotic places, including some in Europe and the Mediterranean. Her favourite in the world, by far is Hawaii.

Being a writer gives her the privilege to explore, travel, and meet wonderful, new and exciting—and sometimes eccentric—people. Her background in English literature, writing, and psychology all help her create unique characters for her stories. Especially her charismatic heroes and feisty heroines who find themselves in sticky situations with each other, their families, and their cultures. There is nothing more satisfying than knowing readers love her warm heroines and the gorgeous enigmatic heroes, as she falls in love with them too.

When she is not painting in various media or watching

romantic movies, or cooking up a storm for her family and friends, she hangs out with her writing friends and other creatives.

Although she was brought up in England, she now lives—and writes—in the Toronto suburbs in Ontario, Canada, with her husband and daughter.

To learn more about the author, visit **www.GloriaSilk.com.**

If you enjoyed this book please consider reviewing it and telling your friends about it.

Partial proceeds of all Gloria Silk's book sales are donated towards cancer research.

Please visit **www.GloriaSilk.com** or email any questions or comments at: **Contact@GloriaSilk.com.**

For More Information visit
www.GloriaSilk.com
contact@gloriasilk.com